Pool Girls

by Cassie Waters

Cool Down

Simon Spotlight
New York London Toronto Sydney New Delhi

This book is a work of fiction. Any references to historical events, real people, or real locales are used fictitiously. Other names, characters, places, and incidents are the product of the author's imagination, and any resemblance to actual events or locales or persons, living or dead, is entirely coincidental.

SIMON SPOTLIGHT
An imprint of Simon & Schuster Children's Publishing Division
1230 Avenue of the Americas, New York, New York 10020

Text by Sarah Albee
For information about special discounts for bulk purchases, please contact Simon & Schuster Special Sales at 1-866-506-1949 or business@simonandschuster.com.
Manufactured in the United States of America 0612 FFG
First Edition 10 9 8 7 6 5 4 3 2 1
ISBN 978-1-4424-4709-7 (pbk)
ISBN 978-1-4424-5377-7 (hc)
ISBN 978-1-4424-4721-9 (eBook)
Library of Congress Catalog Card Number 2011939799

Chapter One

New bathing suit? Check.

Latest issue of *Rocker* magazine, to show that she was as hip as the next girl? Check.

Expensive new leather flip-flops that she'd conned Dad into buying for her, knowing Mom would say no? Check.

Hottest guy in the Western Hemisphere just outside, who might just possibly, finally, notice she was alive? Check. Christina smiled ruefully. Of course Mike was out there. He was on his zillionth lap of the day, no doubt.

Christina did a little twirl in front of the locker room mirror, since no one else was in there. Yes, she had to admit, she looked pretty good in her new metallic-silver tankini, and she was having a great hair day. She clicked on her phone for perhaps the seventeenth time that day to reread Veronica's text from last night:

I asked MM if he liked anyone. Don't be mad. He said maybe kind of sort of but he wasn't positive. Progress?

Christina sighed. It was hard to know where things stood with Mike Morris. He was definitely the Strong, Silent Type. But she considered Veronica's text a step in the right direction.

She opened her bag to put her phone away when it buzzed in her hand. She clicked on the message. It was from Veronica.

Bad news. Sit down before you read my next text.

Christina stared at the text and then slowly lowered herself down onto the bench as though it were a too-hot bath. She texted back:

OK. I'm sitting. What?

The phone buzzed almost immediately.

I'm out here on the pool deck and so is MM. He's brought a friend. A girl.

Christina blinked at the words on her phone screen. That couldn't be possible. Veronica must have it wrong. Yesterday Mike had asked her if she'd be out at the pool today. That was as close as he got to asking her if she wanted to hang out with him. Why would he show up with another girl? There had to be some reasonable explanation. She texted Veronica:

OK, thanks. I'll do some recon before I come out. C U soon.

She took a deep breath and stood up. Only one way to find out—she'd have to spy. In the bathroom area there was a high window, and it looked right out onto the pool. After peering under the stall doors to be double sure no one was in there, she brought a chair over and stepped onto it, stood up carefully, and leaned toward the wall so she could see out.

She didn't have a great view, but she could definitely see at least a third of the pool. Mike wasn't in any of the lounge chairs. Knowing him, he'd be in the water. She waited. Moments later, a swimmer powered across the pool and came to a stop at the end. His shiny brown head emerged and he swept his wet hair out of his face. It was Mike. She would know those muscular arms anywhere. He was talking to someone out of her sight line. Now he was laughing. He usually didn't laugh that hard. Here came another swimmer, someone under the water. A head popped up, long blond hair, shining like diamonds in the bright sunlight. It was a girl. Christina watched as the girl dove back under the water, popped up again right next to Mike, and tried to push him down into the water by his shoulders. Laughing again, he casually peeled her delicate hands off his shoulders and playfully shoved her to the side. Now they were both laughing.

She heard the door open in the other room. Someone was coming into the locker room. Christina scrambled down off the chair, hurried out of the bathroom area, and nearly ran smack into Grace Davis.

"Oh!" said Grace, taking a step back and regarding Christina. "Hi."

"Hi," said Christina. Her thoughts were whirling. Grace was the last person she felt like seeing at a time like this. After the big fight the two old friends had a few weeks ago, they'd barely nodded hello to each other since, and

Christina was not exactly in the mood for idle chitchat with her right now.

"You okay?" asked Grace as she smoothed her hair out in the mirror. "You look a little . . . upset."

"Oh, I'm fine," replied Christina.

Silence.

"Hi, Grace! Hi, Christina!" Kimmy came into the locker room with her little sister, Emily. Kimmy was one of the younger girls on the swim team. Emily looked about six. "Hey, Grace, congratulations on winning Best New Diver at the swim team banquet last week."

Grace smiled, her braces glinting. Christina wished for her sake Grace would go for a different band color than green. It just seemed so, well, childish.

"Thanks, Kimmy," said Grace. She shot Christina a look. Christina didn't care. She wasn't about to congratulate Grace. Grace's head was way too big already, after all the praise she'd gotten for her diving talent this summer.

"So are you guys just hanging out together today?" asked Kimmy.

"No," said both girls at the same time.

"I'm meeting Veronica here," said Christina. "She's leaving for vacation in a couple of days. Along with the rest of the universe," she added bitterly. It was true. Besides

Grace, Christina felt like the last girl on earth not to be on vacation. Everyone was away. She'd been getting giddy text messages from both Ashley and Lindsay, her friends from school, who were at their respective fabulous beach houses and who seemed to be having the best summers of their lives. It hadn't been so bad when she'd thought she might have Mike Morris to spend quality time with. But now everything looked bleak. And even Grace had more of a life than she did—she always seemed to be with her sort-of boyfriend, Justin.

"I'm looking after Emily today," said Kimmy, rolling her eyes. "Come on, you. Let's get changed. See you guys." Kimmy proceeded into the dressing area with her sister.

Grace and Christina stood there awkwardly. Finally Grace spoke. "Justin and I are working on some new dives today."

Christina nodded, but she couldn't come up with anything to say about diving. More silence. "Well, guess I'll be going," said Christina, turning to leave.

Veronica burst into the locker room. "So did you see her?" she asked Christina, then noticed Grace. "Oh! Hey, Grace! I didn't know you were here! Congratulations again on your award!"

Grace smiled. "Hey, Veronica. Thanks. Congratulations to you, too. I think our winning the medley relay might just be one of the high points of my life so far. Who are you talking about?"

Christina cringed inwardly. Grace could be so annoying sometimes. Couldn't she see that this might be a private conversation between her and Veronica?

"Mike Morris showed up with a superpretty girl," said Veronica to Grace. "They're out in the pool together right now. I've never seen the guy look like he's having this much fun." She darted a glance at Christina, as though she just realized what she'd said might have been insensitive. "Sorry. I just meant . . ."

"It's okay," said Christina. "Whatever. Let's go see what's going on."

"All right," said Veronica. As she opened the locker room door, she turned back to address Grace. "Hey, Grace. My dad is letting me treat my friends—what's left of them not on vacation, that is—to lunch at the snack bar tomorrow. Are you around? We can have all the curly fries we can eat!"

Grace looked thrilled. "Sure!" she said. "I'd love to."

"Awesome," said Veronica. "Feel free to invite Justin if you want."

Grace smiled gratefully. "Thanks, that's nice of you. I'll ask him." She flung her bag over her shoulder and headed further into the locker room. Christina felt relieved. Now it was time for her and Veronica to scope out the Mike situation together.

Chapter Two

Now what are they doing?" asked Christina. She and Veronica were out next to the pool, lying side by side. Christina was on her stomach, pretending to read her magazine. Veronica was on her back, pretending to lounge with her eyes closed, but her dark sunglasses allowed for ideal scoping. Christina had put on her own dark glasses as she walked out to the pool, so she could check the new girl out without being too obvious. The girl certainly was pretty. Slim; blonde; a silvery laugh.

"They're having some sort of contest," said Veronica. "I think to see who can swim the farthest underwater. Three guesses who wins every time."

"Where did she *come* from?" said Christina. "I've been

here all summer and have never laid eyes on her!"

"No clue. Now they're cracking up again," said Veronica. "I don't know anything that's *that* funny."

Christina groaned softly. "He never laughs around me," she muttered. "He—"

"Shhh! They're getting out of the pool!" hissed Veronica. "They're coming over here!"

Christina swiveled around and sat up in her lounge chair. Sure enough, Mike and the girl were headed their way.

"Hey, guys," said Mike as they approached. "Want you to meet someone. This is Nikki Angelo. She's my—ow!"

Nikki nudged him to shut him up and then smiled what Christina's dad would call a 10,000-watt smile. Her teeth seemed impossibly white and straight. She shook Veronica's hand and then Christina's. "Hey!" she said. "So psyched to meet you! I was starting to think you had to be, like, over eighty years old to belong to this club. There seem to be no kids around at all!"

Christina forced herself to smile as naturally as she could. "Oh yeah," she said with a strained laugh. "I guess a lot of people have gone off on vacation already."

"Well, I just got *back* from vacation," said Nikki, coiling her long, wet hair expertly into a topknot. Christina was fascinated to find that it stayed put on top of her head and wished she could ask her how she'd done it. "I've been in Paris all summer with my aunt," she said. Nikki sat down on the empty chair next to Veronica. She had on a one-piece, but somehow managed to look totally awesome. Not awkward at all like Christina sometimes felt in her bathing suits.

"Paris?" repeated Veronica. "No way! I was just there over spring break! Do you speak French?"

"Mais oui!" said Nikki with a musical laugh. Christina listened to the two girls compare notes about Paris, feeling somewhat betrayed by Veronica's obvious enthusiasm to talk to Nikki.

"It's the latest thing in France," Nikki was saying to Veronica. She was talking about her adorable, patterned bathing suit. "Every French woman is wearing this style right now."

All Christina could feel at that moment was envious of this incredibly lucky girl. She'd never even been to Canada, let alone Europe. Maybe if her parents hadn't separated, they might have taken a family trip there, but no such luck.

"So do you go to Central Middle School or something? Veronica and I go to Lincoln. I don't think I know you from school, do I?" asked Christina.

"I go to Shipton Academy with Mikey-poo," said Nikki.

Mikey-poo? Barf! Christina couldn't imagine anyone on the planet getting away with calling Mike such a name. But he didn't seem the least bit bothered by it.

"I'm almost always away in the summer," Nikki continued. "That's why I've never been here before. Last summer I went to the Italian Riviera. *Molto bella!*"

"Hey," said Mike, giving Nikki's foot a little nudge with his own. "We have to split. Remember we have to be you-know-where pretty soon."

"Oh! Right!" said Nikki, springing to her feet. "Almost forgot! What would I do without you, Mikey?" She gave a pouty little smile that made Christina's insides churn. "It was so great to meet you guys! See you soon, I hope!"

Veronica and Christina both smiled and waved and watched the two of them head off, shoving each other back and forth as they walked. The two girls lay there in silence for a minute.

Then Veronica spoke. "*Mikey-poo?* She did *not* just call him that."

Christina nodded miserably. "She did."

More silence. Then Veronica spoke glumly. "Her bathing suit was pretty nice, huh."

"Yep."

"Do you think she highlights her hair?"

"Nope. Looks natural."

"Looks good." Veronica sighed. "Sorry, Christina."

Chapter Three

Later that afternoon, Christina sat on the stone wall in front of Riverside Swim Club, swinging her legs and banging the wall semipainfully but not caring, waiting for her mom to pick her up. On her way out she'd seen Grace and Justin sitting together at a snack bar table, their heads bowed together, talking and laughing. She couldn't swear to it, but she was pretty sure she'd seen them holding hands under the table. Grace Davis! Christina would not have predicted in a million years that shy, oh-so-unfashionable Grace would have a regular boyfriend before she did. Her misery deepened. She was the last girl on the planet not to have a boyfriend.

A minute later, her mom pulled up. Christina hopped

down and threw open the car door, then plopped into the seat next to her mom.

"Hi, darling!" trilled her mother, who, irritatingly, did not notice that Christina was in a morose state of mind. Christina took her time clicking into her seat belt, but even that didn't seem to annoy her mother as it usually did. She just sat staring straight ahead, humming absently to the song she was listening to on the oldies station—something from the eighties—a small smile playing on her lips.

"What's up with *you*?" demanded Christina. She knew she was being disagreeable, but she didn't care. What right did her mom have to be so cheerful, anyway? The divorce had gone through a few months ago, her job as a real estate agent was stressful, and she seemed always to be talking on the phone in angry whispers to Christina's dad about money stuff.

Her mother turned to her and smiled. "Hmmm?" she said. "Oh, nothing. How about you?"

Christina glowered down at her fluorescent-pink fingernail polish and shrugged. "Nothing. Everything's fine."

A year ago Christina might have confided in her mom. She might have told her all about Mike and how he'd shown up with a new girlfriend and broken Christina's heart, and her strained relationship with her ex–best friend, Grace, and her loneliness at feeling like the only middle school kid she knew who was not going away to somewhere fun for vacation, let alone without a boyfriend. But now she was getting older. Too old to cry to her mommy, that was for sure.

"I made you some tabbouleh and carrot bread for dinner," her mom said.

Usually, Christina liked this dinner, but for some reason she didn't feel like staying home. "Um, that's great, but I have a counteroffer. Why don't we go to Thai Gardens tonight?" she asked. "I could really use a good dinner out after the lousy day I just had."

"Sorry, honey, I can't. I have plans," said her mom. The song changed to another ancient oldie, and her mom actually started swaying back and forth in her seat to the beat. Thank goodness no one was around to see that. *There should be a law against moms dancing,* Christina thought.

"What plans?" demanded Christina.

"Oh, just . . . plans. Actually, I'm having dinner out tonight."

Christina turned and blinked at her mother. "Like a date?" Her bad day was steadily getting worse.

"Well, no, not really a date," said her mother, a

defensive tone creeping into her voice. "I'm just having a grown-up dinner, is all. It's going to be an early night, though. I'll be home before you go to bed. You can watch a movie in my room if you like."

Christina turned and stared out the window at the passing landscape. It seemed that everywhere she looked she saw couples in love. They passed a young couple on a bench, waiting for a bus. They passed an old man and woman, holding hands and walking with canes. She even saw two dog walkers meet up from opposite directions, their dogs straining at the leashes and greeting each other like long-lost true loves. Her own mother was having a more exciting social life than she was. Yes, this was going down in history as one of the worst days of her life.

Chapter Four

"This is awesome of your parents to treat us to lunch," said Grace, as she, Christina, and Veronica sat down at a table for four, laden with burgers, fries, cold drinks, and salads.

"Yeah, once in a while my parents really come through," Veronica said with a grin. "So, Grace, is Justin coming?"

Grace rolled her eyes. "He said he would. He and Jasper have to help clean up their yard for a big family get-together or something, so he said he might get here late. He's been acting really weird lately, always talking about family time and stuff."

"Where are you going for vacation, Vee?" asked Christina, biting into a deliciously greasy curly fry. Then she sprinkled a bit more salt on the rest of them.

"The shore," said Veronica. "Can't wait."

"Hey, don't look now, but there's Mike and that girl," said Grace, gesturing with her chin toward the snack bar counter, where Marty was whirring smoothies in a blender.

Christina felt her heart flip-flop. She was sitting with her back to the snack bar counter, but she glanced quickly behind her. Sure enough, there were Mike and Nikki, talking and laughing with each other. Nikki was actually standing there with her elbow perched on Mike's broad shoulder, waiting for her smoothie. She had on a simple but perfect-looking sundress and a pair of wedge sandals that made her already long legs look even longer.

"Hey, guys, sorry I'm late," someone behind them said.

Christina turned around and squinted at the person silhouetted by the bright sun. It was Justin McGee. He plopped into the chair between Grace and Christina.

"Hey," said Grace, smiling shyly at him. Her eyes were shining. It struck Christina that Grace really, truly liked Justin. A part of her roiled with jealousy. "I got you a double cheeseburger and curly fries."

"Thanks, I'm starved!" said Justin. "My dad decided Jasper and I had to pull every blade of grass from between the paving stones on the patio. Really pleasant in the beating sun. And it absolutely ruined my perfectly manicured nails."

Grace giggled.

"Hey, look! There's Mike and Nikki," said Justin.

"How do you know Nikki?" Grace started to ask when Justin jumped up, put two fingers into his mouth, and whistled quickly. Mike and Nikki, who had just paid for their smoothies, turned toward the sound. (Had Mike paid for Nikki? Christina couldn't tell.)

"Morris! Over here!" yelled Justin.

Mike and Nikki came over to their table. Justin pulled over two empty chairs, and everyone squeezed together around the small picnic table.

"Hi, you guys!" squealed Nikki, shoving aside Grace's hamburger to set down her smoothie. "Mike and I just stopped by for a quick snack—how awesome to find you here!"

Christina darted a glance at Mike, then looked quickly away. What if Nikki saw her looking at him That Way?

"Is that French?" asked Veronica, gesturing to Nikki's dress. "It's so fab."

"Thanks. Yes, my aunt bought it for me. We were shopping on the Rue de Faubourg Saint-Honoré," said Nikki.

Christina had no clue what Nikki was talking about, but

it certainly was impressive the way Nikki could roll her *r*'s. And Christina knew her fashion. Nikki definitely had a cool sense of style. She stared down at her fries, which were suddenly making her feel sick to her stomach. "Be right back," she said, pushing out her chair and heading for the locker room.

Inside the cool, dark changing room she felt a little better. She went over to the sink area and splashed cold water on her face, not even caring that it might wash away her carefully applied bronzer. She was still leaning over the sink with her eyes closed when she heard a tiny rustle behind her.

"You like Mike, don't you." It was a statement, not a question, and it came from Nikki, who had somehow managed to follow her into the bathroom without making a sound.

Christina whirled around to face her. "I—what are you talking about? No," she stammered lamely.

Nikki stood there, hands on hips, chin lowered, her huge blue eyes boring into Christina. "Admit it. You like him. It's written all over your face."

"I that is, I guess I sort of *did*," said Christina, her voice trembling ever so slightly. "But I didn't know about you. I swear."

Nikki crossed her arms and paced a bit, as if contemplating Christina's words. Then she turned to Christina, her eyes now flashing. She looked like a police interrogator on one of those TV detective shows. "You didn't know about me?" she demanded. "You didn't know about me," she stated, as though pondering her own question. "You didn't know"—she paused dramatically—"that Mike and I are *cousins*?"

Nikki's words floated across the room and into Christina's consciousness. Her brain didn't seem to be processing at its normal pace. At last the meaning registered. Christina looked at Nikki. Nikki was smiling broadly.

"Cousins?" asked Christina.

Nikki nodded, then burst into peals of laughter. "I had you going, though, didn't I?" she said, gasping for air. "You thought we were boyfriend and girlfriend, didn't you? That is kinda gross and so hilarious!"

"Well, yeah, I did, I mean, who knew you guys were cousins? You have different last names, for starters, and you have blond hair and blue eyes, and he's dark and—"

"Mike's dad and my mom are brother and sister," Nikki said, cutting her off. "And lots of Italians have blond hair, although I'm only half-Italian, and also, between you and me, I add highlights to mine. I had these done in Paris." She smiled sweetly at Christina. "Hey, got another idea for you. How about if we don't let on to Grace for a little while about who I really am?"

"Um, I guess so," said Christina. "But why?"

"Well, see, Justin and I used to go to the same school, before I switched to Shipton last year. So I've known him for a couple of years. And also he and Mike are friends, so we've hung out a little from time to time. And last summer we were at the same soccer camp and we kind of went out, for, like, one day. I highly doubt Justin has told Grace about us. And Mikey told me Grace is all into diving. So maybe we could pretend like I'm a really great diver to make her, you know, a little worried." She smiled conspiratorially at Christina. "In actuality I don't have a clue how to dive. Soccer is my sport."

Christina had never been a huge fan of psyching people out, but her relief at finding out that Nikki was Mike's cousin made her want to like Nikki. It was also a little thrilling to do something "bad." Anyway, it was just harmless fun. "Okay, I won't give anything away," she said.

"Great!" said Nikki, her eyes shining. She held up a hand to high-five Christina.

Christina high-fived her back. Her emotional state had just swung around 180 degrees, and she was feeling a little giddy. "So, are you into swimming?" she asked Nikki.

"Psssh, no. I spend too much time on this"—she flipped her shining hair with one hand and gestured to her flawlessly made-up face with the other—"to wash it away in the pool."

"I know what you mean!" said Christina. "Why ruin a perfect hair day, right?"

Nikki threw her arm around Christina, and the two girls walked out of the bathroom together. Christina felt like a weight had been lifted off her. Mike didn't have a girlfriend. Plus, it was awesome to find someone who wasn't completely into swimming, the way the rest of them all seemed to be. Christina wondered if Nikki liked to act and sing, the way she did.

Back at the lunch table, Justin and Mike were talking about a video game or something when Nikki cleared her throat loudly to get them to pay attention to her. "So I was just telling Christina," she said, "that when I was in Paris all summer I went to a diving school run by French Olympic divers! It was awesome. I am, like, so much better than I was last year."

Mike crossed his arms and frowned, but he had an indulgent look on his face, like he was used to Nikki's wild stories.

"Wow! That is amazing!" said Veronica. "So maybe you

can join the team next summer! We can totally use another great diver, right, Grace?"

Justin looked confused, but was clearly unwilling to contradict Nikki. Grace looked worried—Christina wondered if she was afraid of getting bumped from the lineup by someone more talented. She wondered how long Nikki would keep this going. Christina shifted uncomfortably.

"Uh, Nik?" said Mike. "You want to tell us all about this diving school? What was the name of it?"

"Oh, it's called *L'École olympique* . . . Divers."

"Uh-huh. And what new dives did you learn?"

"What dives? All the hardest ones, of course."

"Like what?"

"Um, the triple axel?"

Grace and Veronica exchanged a baffled look.

"Aw, knock it off, Nik," said Mike. He turned to Grace, Christina, and Veronica. "Nik and I are cousins, in case you were wondering. And she's never dived a day in her life, except maybe into my Halloween candy."

"Aw, Mikey, you wrecked the joke!" Nikki said with a pouty look. But the tension around the table immediately lifted. Christina noticed that Grace looked relieved.

Veronica stood up. "Time for me to go," she said. "We're leaving for the shore tonight, and I need to pack. I'll be back before Labor Day, for the end-of-summer party, though."

Christina and Grace hopped up, hurried to give her a hug, and thanked her for lunch. "Have an awesome time!" said Christina, trying to sound as cheerful as possible. Inside all she could think about was how she was down to zero friends to hang out with at RSC now. As they hugged, she looked over Veronica's shoulder at Nikki, who was gathering up her stuff. Nikki caught her gaze and gave Christina a wink. Hmm. Maybe there *was* one person to hang out with after all.

Chapter Five

Wednesday morning, Christina took a gloomy bite of toast as she read and reread the back of the cereal box. She'd tossed and turned much of the night, thinking about Mike. Did he see her as anything more than just a girl who went to his pool? She had awakened at five, lain there for a while, and then finally realized it was pointless to try to get back to sleep and had come downstairs. Her mother seemed to have overslept. What was going on? Two nights in a row she'd gone out to dinner!

Her mom came into the kitchen singing a few minutes later, already dressed for work. "Hello, honey," she said, kissing the top of Christina's head.

Christina didn't even turn around.

"Are you going to the pool today?" her mom asked.

"Yep," said Christina.

"And your father will pick you up there this afternoon, right?"

"Yep," said Christina.

"Do the two of you have anything planned for tonight?"

"Nope."

Her mom set down the bag of coffee she was scooping into the grinder and turned to Christina. "What's up with you today?"

Christina just shrugged.

"Are you upset that I went out last night?"

Christina drew in a deep breath and let it out slowly. Then she turned toward her mom. "Well, it is a little weird that you chose to go out two nights in a row, especially when I'm spending tonight at Dad's. So that makes three nights in a row you seem to be content to live without my company."

Her mom pressed her lips together as she turned on the grinder. When it was finished, she said, "Christina, you know I love you, but I am allowed to have a life. You're old enough to stay home by yourself now, and it's nice for me to be able to go out with adults every now and then."

Christina narrowed her eyes. "Was it . . . with a *man*?"

Her mom started to say something, and then stopped. "Actually, yes. We were going to meet another couple, but they had to cancel, so it just ended up being the two of us. So I suppose it *was* a date." She dumped the ground coffee into the machine and flicked the switch. "It's a man I've been getting to know for a while now. I would like you to meet him."

Christina must have involuntarily given her mother a look because her mother continued, "Now, don't look at me like that, Christina. His name is Nathan, and he has two boys around your age. He and his wife got divorced when the boys were very young."

Christina's mind was rapidly calculating. What if her mom married this guy? Would she have to *live* with two *boys* that she wasn't even *related* to? *Ugh!*

Her mom was still talking. "And he's having a barbecue next week, and I'd like us both to go."

"When?" Horror was written across Christina's face.

"Wednesday."

"Oh well, that's that, I guess," said Christina with relief. "Wednesday is my night with Dad, so you'll have to go without me."

"Actually, no. Your father and I talked about it. You have a dentist appointment next Tuesday, and I'm going to be very busy at an open house, so he agreed to take you. So you'll basically switch your day with your father from Wednesday to Tuesday. We can go together to the party Wednesday night."

Christina groaned inwardly. A party with some old guy dating her mom, where she knew no one and had to make pleasant conversation with a couple of boys who might or might not someday have to share a bathroom with her? Not her idea of the world's funnest evening. But her mom looked so hopeful, almost like she was begging Christina to let it work.

"Okay," Christina said in a low voice. "I'll *try* to be pleasant."

Her mom hugged her. "Thanks, sweetie. You're really growing up so fast. You've become so mature. Now I have to get to the office. I have three new listings to show today."

As her mom busied herself pouring the coffee into a Thermos and wiping down counters, Christina's phone buzzed. It was a text from Nikki:

You want to come to lunch with me today?

Christina texted back:

Yessss! At RSC?

Nikki responded:

No not at RSC—we're going fancy. Meet at La Grenouille at 12:30. You can walk there from RSC. And don't worry about $$, it's on my dad!

Christina felt a thrill of excitement. Nikki was reaching out to her! How amazing to have a fun, fashionable new friend drop out of the sky, just when she thought the rest of the summer was going to be dull and awful, with no cool people to hang out with! And La Grenouille! It was a little French restaurant she'd passed a million times but had never been to. Her phone buzzed. It was Nikki again.

BTW I invited my big lunk of a cousin to come with us. Hope u don't mind.

She almost dropped the phone. Mike was coming! Nikki was helping the two of them get together! What an amazing, awesome, incredible person she must be! It was all Christina could do not to whoop out loud, but she wasn't about to let on to her mother what was going on. Taking a deep breath, she typed:

Awww man, does he have to? JK LOL. Psyched!

Was that cool and casual enough? She decided it was and hit send. Then she bounced in her seat a bit while she waited for the reply. It came right away.

I figured you wouldn't mind! See you L8R

Her mom picked up her bag and keys. "Well, you look like you've perked up a bit. I'm glad to see that. So you'll be at RSC all day until your father comes to get you, yes?" she asked.

Christina looked up from her phone, flustered by her mother's question. "Uh, yep! Yes, I will."

She wasn't sure why she didn't tell her mom about the lunch. She'd probably say yes if Christina asked. But somehow it felt invigorating to make her own decisions.

"All right, honey! Have fun!"

Christina had never kept stuff like this from her mother before. She actually liked having her mom know where she was at all times. It made her feel safe and secure. Well, her mom had complimented her on how grown-up she was becoming. Maybe this was a sign of her maturity.

Chapter Six

By noon the late-August air was already so humid, the sidewalks shimmered and strands of loose hair were sticking to the back of Christina's neck. She walked into RSC with shorts on over her bathing suit bottom. But in her tote bag she had packed her nicest sundress, which she'd convinced her dad to buy for her at the beginning of the summer. Today was the perfect day for the dress—hazy, hot, and humid. She made a beeline for the locker room to change. She'd spent a lot of time on her makeup and on arranging her hair in a topknot, and she had to admit it looked pretty good. She put on the dress and then looked at herself in front of the full-length mirror. The dress was coral-colored with a halter neckline. It draped beautifully in the bodice and accentuated her slim waist and long legs. She did a twirl. She was going to lunch at a fancy restaurant with Mike and Nikki!

She stashed her bag with all her stuff in a locker. She'd change back into her shorts later, when her dad came to pick her up at the club. Although that was probably an unnecessary precaution, 'cause her dad never noticed what she was wearing.

As she emerged from the locker room she saw Grace and Jaci Clifford talking with Justin and Jasper. Grace and Justin were in their bathing suits, and judging by the goggle rings around their eyes and their wet hair, Christina figured they'd been swimming all morning. Jaci and Jasper didn't look as though they'd been in the water at all, which didn't surprise Christina.

"Hey, Christina!" said Grace. "Why all dressed up?"

Christina cringed inwardly. Could Grace ever just be smooth? "Oh, this old thing?" she said as she approached them, flinging her skirt casually. "I've had this for ages. But it's the coolest thing I have to wear in this heat."

"*This* is the coolest thing I have to wear," said Justin, plucking at his wet bathing suit.

"You look like you're not planning on going swimming today," Grace said to Christina. She phrased it as a statement, but it was definitely a question.

Christina could tell Grace was dying of curiosity. She knew her expressions so well. "Maybe in a while," she said. "I have to go, uh, grab a book for my mom from the library. See ya." She headed off toward the main entrance. She could feel Grace's eyes following her, and knew from the look Grace had given her that she hadn't believed her story. Oh well.

A tiny bell tinkled as Christina pushed open the heavy, plum-colored door of La Grenouille. She was immediately engulfed in a cool, hushed atmosphere, so welcome after the humidity outside. It felt like she was stepping into a completely different world. Some French-sounding accordion music was playing softly in the background, and she heard the clink of glasses behind a curtain. She blinked in the sudden dim light, looking for Nikki and Mike. *Please let them be here already. Please let me not be the first one to arrive,* she thought desperately.

"May I 'elp you?" asked a man standing behind a menu on a heavy wooden pedestal. He had shiny, slicked-back hair and wore a dark suit with a purple tie and matching purple hankie peeking out of his breast pocket. His expression was neither rude nor especially welcoming.

"I, um, I'm meeting someone here," said Christina, panic rising in her throat as she realized they weren't there. What if Nikki had just been kidding with her? She seemed to be the sort of person who liked to play practical jokes on people. What if they weren't coming at all? What if she had gotten all dressed up for nothing? What if—

"Christinaaaaaah!" The bell tinkled as the door behind her opened and Nikki and Mike walked in. Mike was as dressed up as Christina had ever seen him, in a striped shirt with a collar and neat khaki shorts. Nikki had on a flowered dress with a twirly skirt. Christina felt relief flood through her as Nikki gave her a big hug. She darted a quick glance at Mike, who plucked at the back of his collar. In addition to looking cuter than ever (and was that cologne she smelled?), he looked like he'd rather be anywhere but here. *Wait, scratch that,* Christina thought. *He would probably rather be in any pool than here.*

"Sorry we're late," Mike said to Christina. "My cousin has never been on time in her entire life."

"That is so not true," said Nikki. "I was *born* a day early. Ask my mom." She turned to the man at the pedestal. *"Bonjour. Trois, s'il vous plaît,"* she said casually.

"I'm guessing they speak English here, Nik," said Mike drily.

Nikki giggled as they followed the man to a booth right near the window. "I know, but it helps me relive my weeks in Paris," she said. "Aunt Geneviève wants me to keep practicing my French. She also thought I should train to become a chef since I'm such a good cook and we both love cooking so much. She's Cordon-Bleu–trained."

"Who is Gordon Bleh?" asked Mike, but Nikki didn't seem to hear.

Christina slid in first. Nikki sat down opposite her. Mike sat down next to Christina.

Mike turned to Christina. "Her aunt 'Geneviève' is actually her aunt Jenny. But Nikki feels the need to Frenchify everything she can."

"Well, maybe if you stuck your head out of the pool once in a while, you might learn a language too, Mikey," said Nikki.

Mike rolled his eyes.

"By the end of July, I was actually starting to *dream* in French," said Nikki to Christina. "They say that's a sign you're completely fluent."

Christina nodded, trying to recover her wits after Mike had chosen to sit next to her, rather than across. She thought about the few phrases of Spanish she'd learned in Spanish class last year. If someone plunked her down in a Spanish-speaking country this very moment, she would not even be able to ask where the bathroom was.

The waiter came over and filled their glasses with water from a glistening silver pitcher that had a white linen napkin tied around it. Christina guessed the napkin was meant to stop any condensation on the sides from dripping onto an important customer. She was growing more and more elated—here she was in a fancy restaurant without any grown-ups at her table, with a highly sophisticated, gorgeous girl who spoke fluent French and wanted to be her friend. And to top it all off, this girl was cousins with the love of her life, who had elected to sit next to her. What an awesome new friend! She noted the color of Nikki's nails—primrose blue, freshly manicured—as Nikki flipped open a menu, and resolved to find the same shade as soon as humanly possible. Nikki's hair was swept dramatically to one side and seemed to swoop around the side of her face effortlessly, with no visible means of hair product support. Her slim, tanned shoulders glistened a bit in the dim lighting, as though she'd sprinkled them with fairy dust. No doubt it was some very expensive French skin cream. She would definitely be incorporating a few of Nikki's fashion accessory ideas into her look when she went back to school.

She didn't dare turn to look at Mike. It would have been too obvious. She studied the menu. It was in both French and English, thank goodness. And they had onion soup—her favorite! It would be perfect—and not too expensive. She wondered how much the prices might matter to Nikki's father. *Soupe à l'oignon,* she thought, preparing to order in French.

"*Trois biftecks avec des pommes frites,*" said Nikki to the waiter, clapping her menu closed and handing it to him. "And please charge everything to my father, Vincent Angelo."

"*Très bien, mademoiselle,*" said the waiter. He collected Mike's and Christina's menus and shuffled softly away.

"What did you order for me?" asked Mike suspiciously. "I'm not eating frogs' legs or snails or anything weird like that."

"Don't worry, Mikey dear, I ordered us all steaks and french fries," said Nikki.

"Oh, just the most expensive thing on the menu," said Mike. He shrugged. "Whatever. I guess Uncle Vin has loosened up a little in his old age."

Christina was secretly disappointed. She'd really wanted the onion soup, but who was she to argue when

Nikki was the hostess? "Will your dad mind that you are charging this to him?" asked Christina.

Nikki laughed and shook her head, so that the little bell earrings she wore tinkled. "He spoils me rotten. He might be a little annoyed at first, but he'll get over it quickly. And anyway, he eats here so often he probably doesn't even look at his statements. I think his secretary pays all his bills."

By the time they were eating their profiteroles (a delicious chocolate pastry thingummy), Christina had vowed to incorporate even more awesome Nikkiesque habits into her own life. She would learn to speak French. She would start parting her hair on the extreme left and would swoop it across to the other side so it fell in softly cascading waves to her shoulders. She would scour the fashion sites for a dress similar to Nikki's.

"I'm stuffed," said Mike. "Can we go now? I need to digest a little and then get a serious workout in before dinner."

Nikki rolled her eyes. "Yes, cousin dearie," she said, patting her lips daintily with the pressed cloth napkin.

Christina did the same. She thought she had pretty good table manners, but who knew what they expected of you in France? She watched as Nikki placed her napkin on the table and then laid her knife and fork neatly together across the side of her plate. Christina did too.

"Hey, do you want to hang out at RSC with me and my bratty little brother tomorrow?" Nikki asked Christina as they emerged into the hot, blinding sunlight. "My mom has a tennis match and needs me to look after him."

"Sure!" said Christina.

"Great. He's nine, but he acts like he's four," said Nikki. "Especially when he gets together with all his bratty little friends."

Mike nodded in agreement, that heart-melting half smile playing on his full lips. "Yeah, he's a big pain all right," he agreed.

Christina could scarcely believe she'd been sitting next to him for the past hour. But had he even noticed her, really? He hadn't said much, but then, he'd been pretty busy chowing down on steak and fries. He'd devoured his own and half of Nikki's. A few times his knee had touched hers under the table. Probably accidentally, but still.

Chapter Seven

The next day, Christina and Nikki lounged next to each other, watching Nikki's little brother, Ben, splashing around with a bunch of other kids.

"This is the life." Nikki sighed, turning from her stomach onto her back and sitting up a bit to survey the scene. "How cool is it to lounge poolside while that extremely good-looking lifeguard watches my brother for me?"

"That's Jordan," said Christina. "He's going to be a junior in high school this year. We all talk about how hot he is."

Nikki shaded her eyes and scanned the water for her brother. "Jordan has blown his whistle about eleven times in the last half hour, mostly at my brother," said

Nikki. "Sometimes I wonder how that kid and I could possibly share the same DNA. Where *is* the kid, anyway?"

Suddenly both girls got drenched by a cascade of water. They both squealed.

"Behhhhhhhn!" yelled Nikki, just as Jordan blew his whistle.

Ben's dark, shiny head popped up from the water. "Oh, sorry, did I splash you guys?" he asked, grinning mischievously and revealing a gap on either side of his mouth where he'd lost teeth.

"No cannonballs!" yelled Jordan, half rising from his chair.

"You are such a little twerp," said Nikki, dabbing herself with a towel and lying back down.

Christina wondered yet again what it must be like to have a brother. Sometimes it was nice to be the only child, but usually she wished she had a sibling, especially a sister. She and Grace had been like sisters, along with their friend Mel Levy, all the way through elementary school.

"There's Grace and Justin," said Nikki.

Both girls watched them as the two headed for the diving platform area of the other pool.

"I don't know what Justin sees in her," said Nikki with a

little sniff. "She has absolutely no sense of style."

"I feel the same way!" said Christina, happy to finally have a partner in fashion again since Lindsay and Ashley had left in early July. "Although, they do have diving and swimming in common," she added, feeling a pang of discomfort at trashing Grace behind her back. But the feeling quickly passed.

Nikki nudged Christina. "Hey," she said. "I have an idea."

Christina felt giddy. Nikki seemed like the kind of person who was full of outrageous ideas and willing to do practically anything. "What?" she asked excitedly.

"I'm going to play a trick on my little brother. He so totally deserves it after that cannonball."

"Okay," said Christina uncertainly. "What kind of trick?"

"Just play along, okay?" She waited until Ben's head popped up from the water. "Hey, Ben!" she called. "Need to talk to you!"

Ben didn't come right away. Nikki had to call him twice more before he reluctantly swam for the ladder and emerged from the pool. He padded over to where the girls were sitting, his arms crossed and a frown on his face. "What?" he demanded. A small puddle of water formed at his feet.

"This is Christina," said Nikki, jerking a thumb at her. "Do you know who she is?"

"No."

Christina had no idea where Nikki was going, but she didn't say anything.

"She's the older sister of that kid you pranked at camp."

Ben's eyes widened slightly, and he regarded Christina with new interest. "I-I didn't do anything," he stammered. Christina thought she detected a hint of fear in his voice.

"That's not what you told me," Nikki continued. "And now the counselors figured out who did it and they told Mom and Dad."

Ben said nothing, but he seemed to have paled beneath his tan.

"So yeah, Dad is leaving work early to come get you and, man, is he mad. He's been talking to the camp back and forth all day, and they're saying they might hold you back a grade at school."

Ben's mouth dropped open.

"Christina here is pretty upset about it all, aren't you, Christina?"

"I, um, well, I—"

"See? She can barely say anything, she's so upset. Anyway, you need to go change pronto and come back here and stand by us and wait for Dad to come for you. I would so not like to be in your shoes right now. Go on. Hurry."

They watched him hurry to the locker room.

"Did you make all that up?" asked Christina.

Nikki giggled. "Yep. I sure have him going, too, don't I? That'll teach him to be a little twerp."

Christina's unease was turning to alarm. "It's a little harsh to keep him in such a state of worry for so long, isn't it?"

"He deserves it. I'll tell him when he gets back. Look. Here he is now."

Ben emerged wearing a shirt over his wet bathing suit, carrying his rolled-up towel under his arm. He came over and sat down on a chair next to Nikki. He stared at the ground, evidently avoiding eye contact with Christina.

"Oh, hey, Ben. One more thing?" said Nikki.

Ben looked at her, his brow furrowed with worry.

"I was just messing with you. Christina doesn't even have a brother. You can go back in the pool."

Ben's eyes flashed. "You're the worst, Nikki!" he hissed.

"Yep, that's me," Nikki said, grinning. "Worst big sister in the world. Now stop splashing us with your cannonballs."

Ben stood up. Christina was surprised to see that he

looked more relieved than angry. She suspected that he was accustomed to having practical jokes played on him. "I'm going back in," he said, and pulled off his T-shirt. He tossed his shirt and towel onto the chair and jumped back into the water. Christina noted he didn't cannonball this time. She glanced at Nikki, who had settled back into her magazine, a satisfied expression on her face. Christina pretended to look straight ahead but eyed Nikki from the side through her dark glasses. Nikki certainly had a mischievous streak in her, that was for sure. She'd never known anyone quite like her. How awesome to have made this new friend so quickly!

Nikki turned toward Christina and lowered her own sunglasses. "Oh, by the way," she said with a wry smile. "I had a little chat with Mike last night. About you."

Christina's heart bounced. She forgot all about Ben. "What did he say?"

"Just stuff. I might have let it slip that you like him."

Christina fell back in her chair. Mortification swirled through every part of her. She was speechless for a second, then scrambled back up and turned to Nikki. "Please tell me you're playing one of your jokes."

Nikki blinked at her and smiled coolly, with a "what do *you* think?" look on her face.

"What did you say?"

"I might have just said something like, 'Hey, you big lunk, did you know Christina likes you?' That kind of thing."

Christina let out an anguished, semichoking noise.

"Well," prompted Nikki, "do you want to know what he said, or not?"

"Yes," said Christina eagerly.

"He seemed really surprised."

"He did?"

"Mmm-hmm."

"Well, so what did he say?"

"Let me think. He said, 'Huh.' You know Mike. He's not one for words."

"'Huh'? What's that supposed to mean?"

"I think it's Mike-speak for 'Gee. It never occurred to me that Christina might like me. I need to think this over.'"

"Oh," said Christina. "So not good, not bad?"

"Give the guy some time to internalize the information. When it comes to swimming, he's a genius. When it comes to females, well, let's say he lacks social intelligence. Ever since we were toddlers, he's been all sports, all the time. It's kind of weird for me to think of him as someone girls could be interested in, but I guess I see why you like him. He does have those big green eyes. Hey!" She sat up again and turned to Christina. "What are you up to next Tuesday?"

"Uh, nothing. Well, oh yeah, I have a dentist appointment at noon, but whatever. Why?" Christina held her breath. Was Nikki going to suggest they do something with Mike?

"A dentist appointment? Blow it off," said Nikki with a dismissive wave of her hand. "That's my sister's day off work, and she can drive."

Christina was a little taken aback at Nikki's bossiness, but she didn't show it. "You have a sister?"

"Yep, older. She's a wild woman and drives my parents crazy, but you'll love her."

"Maybe I can meet her and still go to the dentist. Will she be coming here to RSC?"

Nikki rolled her eyes. "It's not about meeting her, silly. She can drive us places! We can go somewhere fun and not tell our parents!"

Christina's eyes widened. She always told her parents where she was going.

"And anyway," Nikki continued, "there's no way it could happen before noon. She's interning for a film production company this summer and is always going to late-night shows and parties and stuff. She *sleeps* till noon on her days off."

"Oh," said Christina. "Well, maybe she could drive us somewhere in the afternoon, after my appointment?"

"That's not enough time to do something fun," said Nikki. "If you just cancel the appointment, we'll have all afternoon to do something. Maybe she can drive us to the mall. We can hang out there and then maybe go to my house or something."

Christina didn't quite know what to say. What would her mother say if she begged her to cancel the appointment? But hanging out at the mall with this supercool new friend—how could she pass that up? "Um, let me get back to you, okay? It's a little complicated because my parents are, well, they're kind of divorced. My mom and dad are switching days next week, and I'm supposed to be with my dad that day, but maybe I can, uh, blow him off somehow."

"Good," said Nikki, lying back down and putting her sunglasses on. "I'm counting on it."

Christina lay there pondering the situation. Really, what was the big deal? Her dad and mom had switched days because they were too busy to deal with her. So maybe she'd make their lives easier and just take responsibility for her own life.

Chapter Eight

In the locker room the next day, Christina found Grace and Kimmy standing side by side in front of the bulletin board, regarding a large, colorful poster. "'End-of-Summer Party,'" Grace read out loud. "Labor Day weekend. I can't believe we're so close to the end of the summer!"

"Yeah," agreed Kimmy. "It's gone by fast."

Christina studied the poster over their shoulders. "It looks like the party is open to kids from other swim teams, too."

Grace nodded. "Jen Cho told me it's the best party of the whole year. Everyone is back from their summer vacations, and it's superfun because everyone knows it's the last bash of the summer."

They stood there awkwardly for a moment. Kimmy

seemed to sense the tension in the air. Finally Grace muttered a "see ya" and then turned and left.

Christina texted Nikki.

What are you going to wear to the end of summer party?

She was sitting on a bench in the locker room. Almost immediately Nikki texted her back.

Can't decide. Have three options. You?

Christina replied:

I'm going to ask my dad to take me shopping this weekend.

Nikki was quick with a suggestion:

Oooh. You should totally check out Rive Gauche! They have the best stuff—all the latest French fashions. I shop there all the time. I saw the cutest dresses in the window the other day!

Christina smiled and texted back.

Awesome! I'll check it out.

Christina clicked off her phone. She had heard of that boutique. It was on a fancy part of Main Street. She'd never gone in, but it looked awfully expensive.

"So, Dad, can you take me shopping this weekend?" asked Christina when her dad picked her up Friday evening. "I have a big, important party to go to in a couple of weeks, and I have to find something to wear."

Her father frowned. "Didn't you just get a dress?" he asked.

Christina sighed patiently. "That was at the beginning of the summer. And everyone has seen me in it." It was the one she'd worn to lunch with Mike and Nikki this past Wednesday, and a bunch of kids at RSC had seen her in it. "There's this store I just want to check out tomorrow. It's supposed to have great stuff." She knew her mother would not take her there in a million years, but her dad could be pretty clueless.

"Listen, punkin, I've been meaning to tell you—I

have to work part of the day tomorrow."

"But tomorrow's Saturday!"

"I know, but I have a patient who is going through a pretty rough patch, and, well, I have to meet with some people about her and talk to her other doctors. But I'll be back for dinner. We can go out somewhere semi-decent."

Christina slumped in her seat and frowned out her window. Her parents seemed to go out of their way to arrange activities that conflicted with her time with them. "How about Sunday, then?" she said. "I think that shop is open Sundays."

"That'll be a definite maybe."

Christina smiled to herself. She knew her dad well enough to know that he'd feel so guilty about working on Saturday, he'd eventually cave.

The shop was small and looked like a fancy lady's bedroom straight out of an old movie, except that it was not in black-and-white. On the contrary, the color scheme was deep pink, with light pink accents. Pink couches faced each other on opposite sides of the narrow space, which was lined along both walls with racks of clothing. The mauve carpet felt plush under her feet as Christina walked in. An impeccably coiffed saleswoman strode toward them, walking expertly in her four-inch heels. She wore a simple gray dress, and was heavily adorned with ropes of expensive-looking costume jewelry. Christina knew, from having studied a number of online fashion sites, that French women were experts at accessorizing. The woman regarded her distastefully, but a split second later her expression changed when Christina's father entered behind her. "Yes, how may I help you?" she asked breathlessly, directing her question at Christina's father rather than at Christina. She sounded not the least bit French, Christina noticed.

"Oh, I'm just looking," muttered Christina. She wished her father was more elegantly dressed—perhaps in a suit with a purple tie and a purple silk handkerchief peeking out of the front pocket—but he had on his usual weekend wear: khakis, sneakers, and a rumpled shirt.

Her father gave the woman a helpless shrug and perched on the edge of one of the pink couches, which was right next to an ornate three-way mirror. He picked up a French fashion magazine, put it back down again, and then took out his cell phone and began scrolling through it. Christina moved along the racks of dresses, almost afraid to touch them. She knew right away that she would probably not find a dress here. But Nikki had recommended it! This must be where Nikki shopped all the time.

She spotted a shimmery gold dress that looked like it tied at one shoulder. She plucked it carefully from the rack. It was gossamer-thin, as lightweight as a hummingbird, and sparkled in the warm lighting. She moved over to the three-way mirror and held it up to herself. "This is pretty," she said to her father.

He put down his phone and peered at her over his half-glasses. Then he leaned over to look at the tag. He coughed loudly. "Uh, I don't think so, punkin," he said.

Christina darted a glance at the saleswoman, who had moved to a discreet distance. But Christina suspected she was listening intently. She peeked at the sales tag. It was more than a thousand dollars. She gasped and hurriedly put it back on the rack. "Let's go," she muttered to her dad. He seemed only too happy to leave.

As they thanked the saleswoman and headed for the door, Christina saw her remove the dress from the rack where Christina had put it and place it back in its proper place, a haughty look on her face. She felt mortified at what her father had said. The woman must have seen the whole thing.

"Who did you say you know who shopped in that place?" asked her father as they headed for the car. "Jackie Onassis?"

Christina had no idea who he was talking about, but she wasn't in the mood to ask. "Just a friend of a friend," she muttered.

"Well, you can tell her from me that she spends way too much money on her clothes," said her father. "She should spend it on more important things, like paying down the national debt." He looked at his watch. "I should get you back to your mother's soon. I'm on call tonight."

As they drove to her mom's, Christina felt a lump rise in her throat. She knew it was wrong to be so materialistic. And she also knew that that gold dress was way too fancy for the party at RSC. She understood how lucky she was to have parents who could afford nice stuff for her. But she still felt mad. That dress had been *soooo* beautiful. She wondered if there would ever be a day when she could walk into a store like that and not have the saleswoman look as though she'd just taken a sniff of milk past its prime. How did Nikki afford it? The saleswoman was probably *friendly* to her. Her parents must be so awesome to let her shop at that place. And they had sent her to Paris for the summer. Nikki was so lucky.

Chapter Nine

By Monday night, Christina still hadn't decided what to do about going to the mall with Nikki and her sister the next day. Maybe she could still make her appointment *and* go to the mall. Nikki had offered to help her look for a dress for the party. That was so tempting. Christina was becoming borderline obsessed with Nikki's clothes. They were just so—right.

Her mom was in another good mood all through dinner (chickpea-and-red-lentil stew), humming as she took the dishes that Christina had cleared from the table. This irritated Christina. It felt—inappropriate. Like her mom was breaking some rule of motherhood. Mothers weren't supposed to have that much fun apart from their kids. It seemed these days that the better her mother's mood, the worse her own became. The phone rang and Christina answered it.

"Hey, Dad."

"Hey, punkin."

"I saw this cool show on TV today, about Paris architecture. Did you know that—"

"Listen—sorry to interrupt, and I really do want to hear about it—but something has come up at work tomorrow. I have to reschedule a patient, and I don't think I can get you to that dentist appointment. Can I talk to your mom?"

Christina stared at the phone in her hand in disbelief, then handed it silently to her mom. She plunked heavily down onto a chair the backward way and clicked on her phone to read her latest text. It was from Nikki:

Did you cancel?

Christina replied:

Not yet. Still working on it.

Nikki wrote back:

Well, if you come to RSC tomorrow, wear your hair in a low bun like I showed you. M told me he thinks it looks cool that way.

Her face flushed. Mike liked her hair up! Nikki had been insisting she wear it coiled up at the nape of her neck, which Nikki said was "very French." Clearly Nikki knew what she was talking about. She texted back:

OK will do.

She smiled to herself, and then ducked her head so her mother wouldn't see her looking cheerful. She'd been carefully cultivating her annoyed mood all evening. She stared back at the exchange. She was definitely flirting with Mike by way of a friend. A major step in the right direction.

Her mother put the phone down with more energy than usual. "Well," she said, her mouth grim. "Looks like your father can't bring you to the dentist after all. I'm going to have to do some major rearranging at the office tomorrow."

"Why don't we just cancel it?" asked Christina quickly. This could be the solution!

"Are you kidding? I had to book this appointment

more than two months ago," said her mother. "It's getting harder and harder to make an appointment at that dentist's office these days. Anyway, never mind. I'll figure something out."

Her mom draped the dish towel she'd been using on the oven door handle and headed into the living room.

Christina continued to sit at the table, staring straight ahead. It seemed her parents were getting busier and busier these days. Was she that much of a burden? *They only have one kid to deal with,* she thought bitterly. But it felt like every little appointment she had was a major production. Well, if she was taking up so much of their precious time, maybe she'd help them both out. She texted Nikki:

I'm in. I'll cancel. See you tomorrow at noon.

The next morning Christina waited until she was pretty sure her mother would have arrived at the office. Then she called the dentist's office and told them she had to cancel the appointment. She'd just skip this one and go to her next one in six months. She'd never even had a cavity, so how bad would it be to skip one stupid dentist appointment?

As soon as she'd made that call, she phoned her mother.

"Hey, Mom, it turns out Dad says he can take me today after all," she said, praying her mother couldn't detect the lie in her voice over the phone line.

"Oh, that's great!" said her mother. "What a relief! I was just about to cancel today's tour, and now I don't have to."

"Yeah, good," said Christina. She couldn't believe her mom didn't hear how fake her voice sounded. Christina was sure everyone in the whole world could have heard she was lying.

"So he'll take you to his house tonight as originally planned, right?"

"Yep."

"Are you going to the swim club soon?"

"Yep, I'm going to ride there just as soon as I clean my room," said Christina. Now why did she have to say that?

"You are really growing up, aren't you?" said her mother.

After they hung up, Christina texted her dad to say she'd be at RSC by late afternoon, and he could pick her up there at six. It was done.

When she arrived at RSC, she already felt hot and sticky from her bike ride. She pulled off her helmet and clicked it to the handlebars and then patted her hair with her fingers to be sure it was still in its bun. She'd spent a ton of time getting it right—no bumps, not a strand out of place—now that she knew Mike liked it better this way. As she walked into the club, she scanned the snack bar area but didn't see Nikki. That was no surprise. Nikki was always late, it seemed, and anyway, it wasn't even quite noon. She spotted someone swimming laps in the lane pool. It looked a lot like Mike. She hadn't seen him all that much since Nikki had spilled the beans about her crush. She hoped he wasn't avoiding her. But then again, she couldn't help but feel a little shy about the whole thing. She'd never crushed this hard on a guy before, and now he knew!

At a shady table, she found Grace, Jaci, and a couple of younger girls from the swim team eating curly fries.

"Hi, Christina!" said Kimmy. She clunked her chair to one side so Christina could sit down.

Christina smiled at her gratefully. Kimmy had followed her around like a puppy for much of the summer, when Christina had been the team's manager. Christina remembered feeling the same way about older girls when she was that age. It was sweet.

"Do you want to come swimming with us? We were about to go in," said Kimmy.

Grace sat back in her chair and crossed her arms. "You don't look like you're planning to swim today, either," she said to Christina, as though daring her to tell them what she *was* planning to do.

Christina shrugged casually. "I might go in a little later," she said vaguely. Then she saw Grace's expression change. Her eyes lit up. Christina turned in her chair. Justin and Mike were approaching. They'd just gotten out of the water, from the look of their hair and their drippy-wet, baggy suits.

The girls all moved their chairs out to make room for the two guys. "That's okay," said Justin. He perched his elbows across the back of one of the empty chairs and then reached for a curly fry. "We're going back in. We just got out to record some split times."

Christina glanced up at Mike. Their eyes locked for a second, and then both looked away quickly. Had she seen him give her a little smile?

"I have to go home soon," Grace said to Justin. "I have an orthodontist appointment, and my mom will kill me if I'm late for it."

Christina shifted uncomfortably in her chair.

"Will you be around tomorrow?" Grace continued. "Want to do some diving tomorrow afternoon?"

"Can't, sorry," said Justin as he stood back upright. "My

cousins are coming over." He hurried after Mike, who was on his way back to the water.

Grace sighed. "It's always something lately," she said glumly.

"Christiiiiiiiinahhhh!" shouted Nikki from the locker room entrance. She strode across the snack bar area to their table. Christina stood up to greet her. "Hi, guys!" said Nikki in a chirpy voice to Grace and the other girls. "So you ready?" she said to Christina.

"Where are you guys going?" asked Kimmy, who was still young enough not to hide her admiration.

Nikki smiled and gave Kimmy a high five. "We've got a girl day planned," she said with a giggle. "Come on, Christina, my sister's waiting."

Grace hadn't said anything, and Christina didn't want to meet her eye. Was she jealous of Christina's new friendship? Disapproving? Christina didn't want to find out. "Bye, guys!" she said, and she followed Nikki toward the exit.

Nikki brushed up alongside Christina as they walked out, almost sending her toppling over to one side. "What's up with Grace's hair?" she asked snickering. "And did you see that color combo she had on? Maybe she should hire a stylist."

Christina felt uncomfortable. Nikki was right about

Grace's lack of color sense, of course, but still . . . a stylist? She changed the subject. "So I went to Rive Gauche on Sunday."

"Wasn't it *amazing*? I can't live without their adorable little T-shirts. I buy them by the half dozen!" said Nikki.

Christina had noticed those adorable shirts, folded into perfect rectangles on a round table. She'd also seen the price tag—roughly the cost of two steak-and-pommes-frites lunches. "I almost bought this fabulous dress," Christina fibbed. "But they didn't have it in my size."

They emerged from the front door of RSC, and Christina looked around for a waiting car. "Didn't you say your sister was here waiting?"

Nikki shrugged. "She'll probably be here in a minute. She said she'd be right back. She had to drop her friends off at their house."

"So, what's her name again?"

"Jessica. She's going to be a senior."

"In college?" Christina asked.

"No, she's only seventeen," Nikki answered.

"Oh," said Christina. "I guess I thought she was in college. You said she was an intern at a film company."

"She's very mature for her age," Nikki continued and then glanced at Christina when Christina didn't respond.

"Oh, don't tell me you're worried about her driving us. The mall is, like, five minutes from here."

Christina *was* worried. She knew that drivers under eighteen weren't allowed to drive nonsiblings. "No, I'm not worried!" she said quickly. What would her mother say if she saw her? She'd throw a fit. Actually, so would her dad. He was really strict about driving and safety stuff. Hence the hairdo-flattening bike helmet.

"She's totally responsible," said Nikki. "And she's going to be eighteen in just a couple of months."

Nikki was right. It was so not a big deal. She had to stop being so childish.

A red sports car pulled up in front of them. The passenger window unrolled and a blond girl leaned over to call to them. "Hey, guys! Hop in!" She revved the engine.

Nikki got in beside Jessica, and Christina climbed into the back, grateful to be in a somewhat safer part of the car.

"You must be Christina!" said Jessica, smiling. "Nikki told me so much about you!"

Christina smiled and said hello. It was excellent to be driving in a car with a high schooler! But out of consideration for her mother, she clicked her seat belt, then gave it a little tug to be sure it was latched.

Jessica turned out to be a good driver. The three of

them prattled away about clothes and movies for most of the drive. They arrived at the mall safely. Christina was annoyed at herself for having been such a worrywart. She was acting worse than Grace! But somewhere, deep in the pit of her stomach, she had to admit she was beginning to feel a little worried—and guilty—for breaking so many rules.

Chapter Ten

"Have fun, you guys," said Jessica.

"Oh!" said Nikki, looking at her sister in surprise. "You're not coming in with us?"

Jessica laughed. "As *if*. It's my day off, remember? Gotta head to Dani's house. You guys have fun."

Christina saw a hint of disappointment flicker across Nikki's face, but it quickly passed. As they got out of the car, she grabbed Christina's arm and propelled her toward the entrance.

Feeling giddy over having broken about ten of her parents' rules, Christina followed Nikki into the mall. A cool blast of air greeted them as they stepped inside. The hushed entrance, with its vaulted ceiling and purring escalators, seemed to beckon to her. She could smell all the new clothes just waiting for her to try them on. Somewhere not far away she could hear a piano playing, and it sounded like a real musician, rather than piped-in music. She absolutely loved the mall.

"I absolutely hate American malls," said Nikki. "They are so much more sophisticated in Paris, of course. But whatever."

"Yeah, I don't really like malls all that much, either," Christina lied. "When in Rome, do as the Romans do, right? So where should we go first?"

Christina didn't dare suggest a store until Nikki had suggested one first. What if Christina were to propose a store that Nikki hated? After all, Nikki shopped regularly at Rive Gauche.

Nikki curled her lip. "I almost never shop here. I have no idea where the semidecent shops would be," she said.

"We could just walk around," said Christina tentatively.

"Hey! Look at that!" Nikki rushed over to a movie poster displayed in a case near the entrance. "*Horror Sisters* is showing. Have you seen it?"

"Um, no," said Christina. Not only had she not seen it; she had not even heard about it. And she didn't like the sound of any movie title with "horror" in it. From the looks of the deranged teenage boy with dripping fangs on the poster, she knew it was not something she wanted to see. Scary movies gave her nightmares.

"Let's go check it out," said Nikki, plucking her by the edge of her shirt and pulling her in the direction of the theater. Christina reluctantly followed.

"What's it rated?" Christina asked as she and Nikki rode up the escalator toward the theater. "I'm not allowed to see anything past PG-13." Christina didn't mention that she could only see PG-13 movies if her parents came with her.

Nikki cocked her head at Christina and gave her an amused smile. "I had no idea you were such a good little girl!" She giggled. "But not to worry. I'm pretty sure it's rated PG-13."

Christina was secretly hoping it would be R-rated. It would make it so easy if they couldn't get in. Plus she still needed to find something to wear to the party. But no such luck.

"Let's buy our tickets now. It doesn't start for forty more minutes," said Nikki. "We can go hang at Cosmetique while we wait. It's right on the ground level, near the escalator."

Christina wondered how Nikki knew where it was if she never went to the mall. Then her thoughts turned to the movie. Time to branch out. To grow up. After all, it had been ages since she'd been to a scary movie. Now that she was older, it would probably not faze her at all. And it was fun, even exhilarating, to do something adventurous, like seeing a movie she wouldn't ordinarily see.

They bought tickets to the one thirty show and then headed for Cosmetique. Christina loved this store. She hadn't been back to it since before the school year ended, when she and Ashley and Veronica and Lindsay had gotten their makeup done. "Want to get our makeup done?" she suggested to Nikki.

Nikki wrinkled her nose. "Not now," she said. "I spent way too much time on mine this morning to mess it all up again."

Christina looked more closely at Nikki's face. She really was talented. Unless you knew what to look for, you'd never guess how much time and effort had gone into achieving her perfectly even skin tone, and the way she'd made up her already large blue eyes to look even larger was practically at the professional level.

"Let's check out the hair colors," said Nikki, once again pulling Christina along. Christina followed her.

In the hair color section, Nikki searched the rack with

a practiced eye. Then she pounced on something on a low shelf and showed it to Christina. "This stuff is amazing on dark hair," she said. "It wouldn't work on me, but it would be gorgeous on you. Should we try it out?"

We? thought Christina. A creepy-crawly feeling skittered up and down Christina's spine. Her mom might never know that she'd seen a scary PG-13 movie, but it would be much harder to avoid her mom noticing dyed hair.

"All the French women tint their hair this color," Nikki was saying excitedly. "It's only a glaze. It won't permanently color your hair or anything. It comes out after, well, after a few washings."

Christina studied the box uncertainly. "My mom would not be pleased. She's one of those all-natural yoga types."

Nikki laughed. "It's so subtle, she probably won't even notice it. And even if she did, she'd get over it. It's not like you're getting a tattoo or something."

Christina laughed nervously. She wouldn't put it past Nikki to suggest that next. Maybe she was getting off easy with just the hair glaze. And the more she thought about it, the more fun it sounded. Why not change her look? Maybe it would be just the thing to get Mike to really notice her! "Okay," she said. "I'll give it a try."

Nikki squealed and hugged her. "I know how to do it. I helped Jess's friend's sister do it a while ago. And trust me: People will think you are French."

Christina nodded and made her way to the register.

When they emerged from the movie, Christina felt that disorienting numbness she always got when she came out of a theater in the daytime. Not sure what time it is, day it is, world it is. She'd hated the movie. It was a pseudo-horror film about two babysitter sisters who get preyed on by a werewolf classmate. She was sure she'd have bad dreams tonight.

"That. Was. Awesome," said Nikki as they headed down the escalator. "Did you love it when the boyfriend took the fireplace poker and—"

"Yeah that was awesome," Christina interrupted quickly. She so did not feel like reliving the movie. "Let's go outside. I need a little air."

"How about if we go to my house?" said Nikki. "It's only two thirty. Your mom will still be at work, right?"

"But I still need to find a dress," Christina said.

"Let's put that off for another day," said Nikki. "I'm beat after all that screaming at the movie."

"How would we get to your house?" asked Christina, looking around for Jessica's car.

"Bus," said Nikki. "I take it all the time. It stops a block from my house. And in Paris I took the Metro everywhere by myself."

Christina felt another rush of exhilaration. She had taken the bus a lot, of course, but only once by herself, and that time, her dad had watched her get on and her mom had been waiting for her at the other end. Why not, though? She wasn't a little kid anymore.

After a rather bumpy ride, the bus hissed to a stop at the corner near Nikki's house, and both girls got off. Nikki lived on a quiet, leafy street with big houses set back from the road. Nikki's house was one of the larger ones, with a huge screened porch. Christina loved the look of it.

"Come on, I'm starving," said Nikki, banging open the screen door and heading toward the back of the house. "My mom's at her all-day tennis clinic, so no one is home." Christina followed her down the hallway, emerging into a large, sunny kitchen with gleaming wood floors. Nikki headed straight for a cabinet, a floor-to-ceiling double door that opened to reveal a treasure trove of snack food.

Christina's jaw dropped. She'd never seen so much delicious-looking junk in anyone's house before. She thought ruefully of her own parents' cupboards. In her mother's there was nothing but healthy stuff like tahini, canned tomatoes, and black beans. And in her father's there was pretty much nothing at all. They usually got take-out. But here there were multiple brands of cookies, chips, salsa, sugary cereals, boxed baked goods, popcorn . . .

"How about if we have an ice-cream sundae?" suggested Nikki, opening the freezer to reveal stacks of ice cream—and not the half-gallon kind but the fancier, pint-size kind. Before Christina could say anything, Nikki grabbed a couple of containers of ice cream and put them on the shining counter, then turned back to the cupboard and started stacking sprinkles, nuts, and chocolate sauce on the counter.

Christina was amazed. In both her mom's and her dad's houses, it was strictly against the rules to have a huge dessert this close to dinnertime. Nikki handed Christina a spoon and the two girls dug in. Christina couldn't help thinking that this might be the best ice-cream sundae she'd ever had. Maybe it was because she was breaking yet another rule.

Chapter Eleven

After their sundaes, Nikki led Christina upstairs to her bathroom. "I share this with Jess but, thankfully, not with Ben," said Nikki. It was definitely a girl's bathroom, with a crowded open cabinet of fascinating makeup and hair and skin products.

She noticed a box of highlighter for blond hair. Hadn't Nikki said she'd gotten her highlights done in Paris? Maybe this was Jessica's. Christina would have loved to explore the products in more detail, but Nikki was busily unpacking the hair kit box.

"Okay, first, here's a T-shirt of my brother's. Put it on. This stuff stains."

Christina looked down dubiously at the shirt Nikki had

thrust into her hands. "Are you sure he doesn't need it? It doesn't look all that old."

"He'll never miss it," said Nikki.

Christina pulled Ben's shirt on over her own. She looked at herself in the mirror. It was odd to see herself in a Boston Red Sox shirt. But she didn't have much time to contemplate her reflection, because Nikki threw a towel around her shoulders.

"Are you sure your mom won't care about this towel?" asked Christina, fingering the plushy material. It looked brand-new.

"We have a gazillion towels," said Nikki, opening a jar of petroleum jelly and dabbing it around Christina's hairline. "This is so it won't stain your skin," she explained. Then she pulled on a pair of clear plastic gloves.

"What are those for?" asked Christina.

"So I don't turn my hands red, silly!" Nikki laughed. She unscrewed the bottle of color and set it down on the sink. Christina peered into it. The ominous, bloodred goo looked like it came straight from the set of *Horror Sisters*. Nikki screwed on an applicator tip. She began squeezing gobs of the gory-looking goop onto Christina's dry hair. Then she took a wide-toothed comb and began combing it through to the ends.

"Okay, now we wait," said Nikki, setting the comb down on a folded-over magazine.

"How long do I keep it on here?" asked Christina, her voice coming out unnaturally high.

"Well, hmm," said Nikki, keeping her goo-covered, gloved hands raised to her shoulders as she peered at the directions. She looked like a mad scientist who'd just performed an autopsy on a vampire that had recently gone on a feeding frenzy. Christina shuddered. "Leave it on for ten minutes and the color will last three to four weeks," she read. "Half an hour makes it last six months. Unless you want a 'vibrant red,' and then we leave it on for a few hours. Should we go for the vibrant red?"

"Um, let's go for the shorter one!" said Christina quickly.

"You're the boss," said Nikki, peeling off her gloves. "Let's go wait in my room. I've got a bunch of new magazines we can read."

Christina smiled—she loved reading the fashion mags with her friends Lindsay and Ashley, and it felt like ages since she'd seen them. She couldn't wait to see what Nikki thought of her favorite designers and celebrities.

Sometime later, as the girls leafed through their second magazine, Christina sat upright in a panic. "What time is it?" she blurted out. "Has it been ten minutes yet?"

"I don't know," Nikki replied. "I haven't been keeping track of the time, have you?"

"No! Oh no!" said Christina, rushing into the bathroom with Nikki on her heels. She hadn't felt such a combination of terror and exhilaration since she'd ridden the Expedition Everest roller coaster at Disney World.

"Okay, I think we should be good," said Nikki. "Let's rinse it."

She offered Christina her elbow and helped her over to the side of the tub; Christina knelt down and turned on the water. She put her head underneath the cascading faucet as fast as she could. Red-tinted water swirled down the drain, and kept swirling. "How long does it take to rinse out?" she asked from her upside-down position. The water was turning from bloodred to medium red.

"You're supposed to rinse until the water runs clear," said Nikki, who was now sitting next to Christina at the side of the tub, reading the instructions. "Then shampoo and condition thoroughly."

Half an hour later, Christina sat on Nikki's bed, her hair twined up in a turban over her head. Her hands were stained pink, and Ben's shirt was hopelessly splattered. "I'm afraid to look at my hair," she said in a small voice. "Will you?"

Nikki no longer seemed as confident as she had before. She just nodded, a solemn expression on her face. Christina unfastened the towel and let her wet hair tumble around her shoulders. She studied Nikki's face.

Nikki cocked her head to one side and eyed her thoughtfully. "Well, it's hard to tell how red it is while it's so wet," she said. "But I think it will turn out okay."

Christina moved into the bathroom and looked at herself in the mirror. She could definitely detect a new reddish hue to her hair. At least it wasn't drastically purple or anything. Nikki took out her round brush and blow dryer and began expertly drying Christina's hair.

"You look beautiful," she said twenty minutes later as she stood behind Christina at the bathroom mirror.

Christina turned this way and that to see her hair at every angle. It really did look nice. Not drastic. Not fluorescent. Just a soft reddish tint to her already dark hair. She bounced up and down excitedly and turned to face Nikki. "Thank you, thank you, thank you!" she gushed. "It does look pretty nice, doesn't it?"

Nikki gave her a big hug. "I'm so glad you like it!"

Christina checked her cell phone to see the time. "I have to get back to RSC. My dad is picking me up there at six."

"I'll text Jessica to see if she can drop you," said Nikki, taking out her phone and texting rapidly.

Christina waited, the feelings of exhilaration and apprehension clashing inside her. Nikki was definitely the most exciting friend she'd ever had, that was for sure!

"Aw, Jess says she can't get back until later. But the bus can drop you right near RSC," said Nikki. "I'll walk you to the bus stop."

Christina put the image of her mother's disapproving face out of her mind as she and Nikki headed to the bus stop. She was totally old enough to take the bus by herself. It was time her parents noticed how much she'd grown up.

Chapter Twelve

Christina's dad was late picking her up at RSC, which for once was a good thing. She'd barely arrived from the bus stop and just had time to unlock her bike and wheel it around to the front of RSC when her dad drove up.

"Hey, punkin, sorry I'm late," he said as he hopped out of the car and hurried around to the back to put the seat down. He gave her a quick peck on the cheek and then finagled her bike at a diagonal into the car, just managing to get the hatch closed. Not surprisingly, Christina's dad didn't even notice her hair.

"How was the dentist?" he asked.

"Uh, good. No cavities." She needed to change the subject fast. "Did you have an emergency at work?" she asked, sliding into the front passenger seat.

"Nah, just the usual backlog of patients to see," said her dad, clicking in and pulling away. "How about Japanese food tonight?"

"I'm not that hungry, actually," said Christina, guiltily recalling the towering mint-chip-chocolate–Moose Tracks–caramel-fudge sundae she'd eaten two hours earlier. "I guess it's the heat and all the exercise I got at the pool today."

Her father seemed disappointed. "Okay, then we can just get pizza and bring it home," he said, handing her his phone to order it. She knew the number by heart.

"What happened to your hair?" exclaimed Grace the first minute she laid eyes on Christina the next day. Grace had been walking past Christina, but she stopped abruptly and stared.

Christina was reclining on the pool deck alongside the water, trailing her fingers in the water and watching the ripples, idly hoping Mike might pass by. She sat up. "I put a semipermanent rinse into it," said Christina. She did not like Grace's tone.

"Oh," said Grace. She stared at Christina's hair and

seemed to be struggling to come up with something to say about it. "It's . . . dramatic."

Christina lay back down and propped herself on her elbows. "That's just because I'm in the sun. It's actually very subtle," she said drily.

"Doesn't she look fabulous?" demanded Nikki. Her head had just popped out of the water, close to the wall next to Christina. Christina noted that Nikki even looked elegant soaking wet. Her dark lashes formed stars that emphasized her huge blue eyes. Christina felt a whoosh of happiness that Nikki had appeared when she did. Her very presence made Christina feel, well, legitimized. Grace just did not get this kind of stuff, and Nikki did.

"Sure," said Grace with a shrug.

Nikki shielded her gaze from the sun and looked up at Grace. "What. You don't think her hair looks *magnifique*?"

Grace faltered. "No, I didn't say—It's nice. Can you swim with that stuff in your hair or does it come out in the pool?"

"Of course she can," Nikki interrupted. "Look, there's my cuz, Christina. Want to come with me to say hi?"

Grace seemed to take the hint. She started to say something, then stopped herself. With a little shrug, she headed off.

"Can you say 'fashion don't'?" Nikki said, chortling. "*What* is she *thinking* with that baggy T-shirt? And those gym shorts with the yellow piping are evil incarnate."

Christina giggled. She knew it wasn't nice to laugh at Grace behind her back, but Nikki really could be funny. And fun. Still, Christina shuddered to think what could happen to her if she got on Nikki's bad side.

"You look a little tired," said Nikki.

"Oh, I was up late last night," said Christina. This wasn't entirely truthful, but she wasn't about to admit to Nikki that the movie they'd seen yesterday had given her nightmares. She'd awakened three times during the night, panting and sweating from scary dreams. No wonder her mom had forbidden her to see horror movies.

"Mikeeeeeeeeey!" yelled Nikki, waving both arms over her head so Mike would notice her as he headed toward them from the other pool.

He turned and waved at them, then made his way over.

Mike pulled a lounge chair over and perched at the end of it. "Hey," he said, jerking his chin upward in his trademark "hello" gesture. He looked at Christina and blinked at her. "What happened to your hair?" he asked.

"Well, I—"

"We were just having a little fun yesterday," Nikki said, jumping in.

Christina smiled and shrugged as if to say, "Who can resist Nikki when she gets an idea in her head?"

Mike seemed to get the picture. He grinned. "Looks cool," he said. "But word of advice: Keep away from this cousin of mine if you know what's good for you."

Nikki beamed, her gaze moving from Christina to Mike and back to Christina. "I'm going to do my laps," she said. "You two don't mind me." And she plunged back beneath the water, her blond hair streaming behind her.

Mike and Christina watched her go. Mike cleared his throat. Christina raked her fingers through her hair, first on one side and then on the other. She pulled up her knees and hugged them, watching the lap swimmers go by.

"So I was just thinking," said Mike.

"Uh-huh?" she said, then immediately regretted jumping in. It made her sound too eager, too desperate. *Keep quiet,* she told herself.

"Yeah, I was just thinking."

Christina kept quiet this time, and she dangled her fingers in the water. They both watched her fingers intently.

"Well, it's supposed to rain tomorrow, but on Friday it's

supposed to be pretty nice, not too hot or anything," he began again.

She flickered her fingers to make the water jump and bump around. She didn't say anything, but her breathing got shallower as she waited to hear what he would say next.

"So, like, would you have any interest in, like, hanging out and maybe going to that new miniature golf place?"

She waited for him to add "with a bunch of kids" or something, but he didn't. It did seem as though he was asking her out, just her, just the two of them, no big group. She drew in a deep breath and breathed out.

"That sounds fun," she said, arranging her face to look calm and making her voice sound casual, which took superhuman strength. "I haven't been there yet, but I hear it's great."

"Awesome," he said, standing back up. "Why don't we meet here at, like, three? We can walk there from here and I think my dad can drive us home."

"Okay," she said, and smiled up at him. As he turned to walk away, she followed him with her gaze. His shoulders were impossibly broad. He looked so mature. Inside, her voice was screaming over and over, *I've got a date with Mike Morris! A date! A date with Mike Morris!* Had the whole world just heard that voice? She darted a look around at the lap swimmers, the little kids in their swimmies, the lifeguard sitting high up in her chair. No, the world was continuing as though everything were normal. She couldn't *wait* to tell Nikki the news! Then again, Nikki probably knew. In fact, it was thanks to Nikki that this whole thing was happening! If Nikki hadn't blabbed to Mike that Christina liked him, Mike might never have realized.

Christina was bursting with joy. She stood up and leaped into the water, not caring about her hair, her makeup, her anything. She needed to do something to channel this exuberance. She loved Nikki! She loved her hair! She loved the world! *She had a date with Mike!*

Chapter Thirteen

Christina floated through the rest of the day at RSC as if in a fog. She hung out at the snack bar with Nikki. Jaci and Grace sat near them at poolside, and Christina and Nikki exchanged surreptitious eye rolls with each other as they heard Grace complain to Jaci that Justin had not even shown his face at RSC today. Grace muttered darkly about "family time." But Christina lost interest in hearing about Grace's woes as she watched Mike swim his endless laps. She whispered and giggled with Nikki. She was dimly aware that Jaci and Grace had begun discussing something serious, their heads bowed together as they talked in low tones, but she paid no attention. It didn't bother her a bit that Jaci had most likely replaced her as Grace's best friend. She had Nikki! And now she was probably going to be dating Mike!

As Christina was clearing her stuff away after lunch, she saw someone emerging from the locker room. It was Jen Cho, the star of the swim team, who'd hurt her leg on the Fourth of July.

"Jen!" yelled Christina. She dumped her trash and raced over to her. "You're back from vacation! You're off crutches! You're not limping!" She gave her a huge hug, then stepped back and regarded Jen with delight. "You look fabulous!"

Jen beamed. "I know. My leg is so much better. I'm swimming again! You look beautiful. Your hair! And, well, you just look so happy!"

Christina bounced up and down and laughed. "Thanks. It's been a great day today." She made a mental note to put on a hat to cover her hair before she saw her mother. She'd brought one with her for just that purpose.

"Do you want to come in the pool with me? I'm going to do some easy laps."

Christina sighed. "Can't, sorry. My mom is picking me up early. We have to go to some dumb barbecue thing tonight."

Jen gave her another hug. "See you soon, I hope."

As Christina walked toward the locker room to gather up her stuff, she caught a glimpse of Mike as he was toweling off near the deck chairs. She smiled shyly at him. He gave her that upward chin jerk, with the half smile that made his dreamy green eyes go all crinkly and practically made her knees buckle.

She couldn't wipe the smile off her face even as she got into her mom's car.

"You look cheerful!" said her mother as she pulled away from the curb.

"Yeah, I had fun today," said Christina, turning to smile out the window.

"Well, good. Keep up that cheerful face awhile longer, please. I'm really excited for you to meet Nathan."

"Nathan? I have to call him that?"

"Well, sure," said her mother.

Christina darted a glance at her mother. She seemed nervous. She'd put a lot of effort into her appearance, even though she looked so casual in a sundress and flip-flops. She must have changed at the office. Her hair was shining and smoothly brushed, and she'd spent time on her makeup. She'd even gotten a manicure. That was weird. Her mom never took the time to get manicures. Christina leaned over and pretended to fuss with the radio while she scrutinized her mother's nails. Yep. Professionally done. Things with this Nathan guy looked serious.

"That's a cute hat," said her mother.

Christina had remembered just in time to put on her pink baseball hat to hide her hair. Now didn't seem like the right time to spring her new look on her mother, given how nervous her mom seemed to be. Christina hadn't bothered to reapply her makeup after she'd been swimming. Who cared? It wasn't like she was going to see anyone she knew at this party.

They pulled into a winding driveway and a large house came into view. Several cars were parked in the paved area near the garage, where there was a basketball hoop and assorted sports stuff scattered around. "This is nice," said Christina. She knew she had to gather herself and act cheerful for her mother's sake. *The thing to do,* she told herself, *is think about Mike.*

"I made hummus with fresh chickpeas, not from a can," said her mother, pulling a bowl and a tote bag from the backseat. She handed the bag to Christina to carry, then opened the door and got out.

As they walked around to the back of the house, Christina could smell chicken grilling and saw a small gathering of grown-ups sitting around at a table. Tiki torches flickered around the perimeter of the patio. It was starting to grow dark already, a sign that fall would soon be here.

A man sprang up from the table and hurried over to greet them. He was tall—taller than Christina's dad—and seemed to be balding, but it was hard to tell, as his hair was closely shorn. He wore silver-rimmed glasses and had dark eyes, practically black. His whole face crinkled into a smile. He looked like he was about to hug her mom, but he hesitated at the last minute and just clasped both her hands in his own. She had to admit, he was pleasant-looking . . . and kind of familiar. He held out a hand and shook Christina's warmly.

"Christina, this is Nathan," said her mother.

Christina knew her mom's tone well enough to know that she was extremely nervous. Time to rally. "Hi," said Christina, smiling up at him with her fake-friendly smile.

"I've heard so much about you from the boys," said Nathan. "They're down there in the field playing Wiffle ball. Why don't you go say hello? We should be eating soon."

Christina looked at him, slightly confused, but didn't say anything. What boys was he talking about? She handed her mom the bag, then made her way through an opening in the hedge and headed down toward the field, where she saw a group of kids playing ball. As she got closer, she stopped in her tracks and stared. Justin McGee was pitching the ball to his twin brother, Jasper.

Justin and Jasper. This was *their* house? Nathan was *their* dad? A coincidence of this magnitude was *not* possible.

"Hey, Christina!" Justin called, tossing the ball off to one side. "Let's finish the game after dinner, guys," he said to the other kids. "I think it's almost time to eat."

Christina just stood there, still in shock, as the group of kids trudged up the hill toward her.

"This is Christina Cooper," said Justin to the other kids. "You know Jasper, of course."

"Hey!" said Jasper. "I met you at RSC. You're friends with Grace, right? And Grace is friends with Jaci. Which makes us friends once removed, right?" He clapped Christina warmly on the back, which set her coughing.

"Yeah, good point, Jasp," said Justin. "Go help Dad with the food, wouldja? So, these are our cousins, Alex, Luke, Sam, Cathy, and the two little ones over there are Owen and Zach."

Still slightly stunned, Christina nodded and said hello, and the rest of the kids headed up to the backyard barbecue area. Justin held Christina back by her elbow and waited for the rest of them to move out of earshot.

"You look upset," he said. "Are you weirded out by my dad and your mom?"

"I guess a little," said Christina. "I had no idea this was your house we were going to."

Justin's eyes widened. "I just figured it out a few days ago. No wonder you look like you've just been socked in the stomach."

Anger at her mother welled up inside her. It was so not fair of her mother not to tell her! She felt blindsided and, well, like she'd been tricked.

They stood there awkwardly in silence. Finally Justin spoke. "Grace has been a little upset with me lately," he said. "I think I was having kind of a hard time with my dad dating too. I finally realized that's what was bothering me. I hadn't even told her about it. I guess Jaci told her the deal today, and then Grace and I had a good talk late this afternoon about it. She really made me feel better about the whole thing. She told me she's known your mom since you guys were really little."

Christina nodded. "We were in preschool together. Our moms are good friends. So are our dads."

"Well, Grace just went on and on about how cool your mom is. She told me your mom is like her second mother.

She made me feel pretty good about my dad hanging out with her."

"That was nice of Grace to say," said Christina. A flood of memories whooshed into her mind, quick takes from her childhood with Grace—their ballet classes, birthday parties, and sleepovers. She'd gone to Grace's gymnastics meets, and Grace had come to all her plays when the two of them were in elementary school.

"I heard about the miniature golf thing," said Justin with a mischievous grin.

Christina's eyes widened. "How did you hear?"

"News that big takes about eight minutes to get around. I'd be shocked if my *grandmother* hasn't already heard about it. Come on. Let's go eat."

After her pleasant conversation with Justin, Christina tried to be cheerful during dinner, but her mood grew gloomier as she observed her mother with Nathan throughout the course of the evening. Her mom was definitely not acting her age. She was behaving like a teenager, all giggly and flirty. It just seemed inappropriate.

Christina glanced at the time on her cell phone under the tablecloth. How much longer did they have to stay? Justin's cousins seemed nice enough, but on the geeky side. Jasper dominated the conversation, yammering away about some bassoon solo he'd nailed at his performance camp. A bunch of the cousins went into the screened-off porch, sat down at an old upright piano, and took turns playing stuff. Some of them were pretty good, but she wasn't in the mood for listening to other kids play. But she also wasn't in the mood to keep sitting with the grown-ups, who were now droning on about Congress or something like that.

She came up with a plan C and excused herself to the bathroom. Once inside, she leaned against the wall and texted Nikki.

This BBQ has turned into quite the evening. So much to tell you!!!

Almost immediately, her phone buzzed.

Can't wait to hear! We're all still at RSC, hanging by the pool. It's awesome. The moon is out. Such a romantic evening. Can you come by later?

Christina texted back.

I wish. But I doubt it. I'll call you later!!

Her misery deepened. She conjured up a dreamlike image of Mike sparkling in the moonlight. Without her. Was it possible he was thinking about her too?

There was a quiet knock at the door. Christina put her phone back in her pocket and unlocked the door. It was her mother. She did not look pleased.

"Step in for a second," she said, pushing Christina back into the bathroom and coming in herself. They stood facing each other. "What is the deal with you?" her mother asked. "You look like you're having a terrible time."

Christina shrugged. "Nothing. Just . . . nothing. I was just a little weirded out to find out this is Justin and Jasper's house."

Her mother nodded grimly, as though she'd expected that answer. "It never crossed my mind that you three knew one another. The twins go to Central Middle School. I had no idea you'd met at your swim club. They just mentioned to Nathan today that you all know one another. He didn't know, either."

Christina frowned. "Whatever."

Her mother's expression darkened. "Christina. I won't have you spoiling my evening. Nathan is a lovely man, and he truly hopes you will accept him as part of my life now. You need to understand that I am allowed to have a life.

You may not like it, but it's the way it's going to be."

Christina narrowed her eyes. "Well, I have a life too, you know. It would be nice for you to take my feelings into consideration. For a change." She opened the door and stalked out. It seemed like everything was disappointing these days. At least she had her date with Mike to look forward to.

Chapter Fourteen

Christina had another bad dream that night. One of the horror sisters was chasing her with dripping fangs, and her feet felt like they were encased in cinder-block shoes, so she couldn't run away. She awoke with a yell, her heart pounding and her body sweating, and then realized she'd been dreaming. "Think of Mike. Think of Mike," she told herself soothingly, and soon fell back to sleep.

It felt like just a few hours later when Christina awoke to the sound of the phone ringing. As the mist of sleep cleared, she realized she heard rain pattering on the roof. Mike had been right about the weather. She turned to look at the clock and groaned. Only seven a.m. Who calls someone's house at that hour? She put her pillow over her head and rolled over, but now she was thinking about Mike and their date tomorrow. She smiled and tried to will herself to fall back to sleep and into a pleasant dream about him. No such luck.

After another fifteen minutes of fruitless attempts to fall back to sleep, she finally sat up in bed, exasperated. With so few days of summer left, why was she waking up voluntarily at such a shockingly early hour? Especially on a day when no one would be at RSC? She had a day of TV and Internet surfing to look forward to. At least she could also dream about her amazing date with Mike, which was now only thirty hours away!

As she came downstairs, she thought she heard voices in the kitchen, a murmured conversation. That was weird. She pushed open the kitchen door. There stood her father, dressed for work in a suit. He leaned against the kitchen counter, his arms and legs crossed, a deep frown on his face. Her mother was over at the coffeemaker, holding two cups of coffee. She put one down next to Christina's dad and then turned to regard Christina.

It was strange to see them here together, in the same room. Except for her school plays and the Christmas concert, she hadn't seen them together in a long time. But she didn't have much time to reflect on that. She did not like the expressions on their faces. They both looked distinctly displeased.

"Um, hi, Dad," she said tentatively.

He didn't answer. He just lowered his chin and stared at her over the tops of his glasses.

Her mother spoke first. "I'm glad you woke up on your own. If you hadn't come down, I would have gone upstairs to wake you."

"I heard the phone ring," said Christina in a small voice. From the tone of her mother's voice, she knew she was definitely in trouble.

"That was me calling," said her dad. "I got home late last night to a message on my machine. It was from the dentist's office. Seems someone canceled your appointment. They were calling to reschedule."

Christina slumped.

"So I called your mother first thing this morning," her father continued, "and we realized you had *lied*." He paused, as if to let the full impact of that word sink in. "First to her, and then to me."

Christina didn't know what to say. Under the best of circumstances, her brain didn't work very well this early in the morning. And this was not the best of circumstances.

Her mother suddenly leaned forward and peered closely at Christina. "What in the *world* did you do to your *hair*?"

Her hair. She'd forgotten about her hair. "Um, I tinted it a teeny-tiny bit? But it's not permanent. It's just . . . well, semipermanent."

"I *thought* it looked different," said her father.

Her mother wheeled on her father. "Different? You didn't notice she'd dyed her hair *purple*, the whole time she was staying at your *house*?"

"We were in dim light most of the time," mumbled her dad sheepishly.

Christina hated when her parents argued. "Anyway, it's not purple; it's red," she said. "You know Dad has always been a little color-blind," she added.

Her mother's voice began to climb. "Never *mind* what shade of *purple* it is. The fact is you *dyed* your *hair* and broke practically every rule in the *house* and—"

"Ava, please," said her dad. "Let Christina give us her side."

"All the French women are coloring their hair like this these days," said Christina in a small voice.

Her parents exchanged a look. Then her mother sat down at the kitchen table and took a deep breath.

"Christina. Please tell us what you did on Tuesday. Did you stay at RSC the whole time? Is that when you did this to your hair?"

Christina thought of answering yes, but she'd already got caught in one lie. She didn't want to get caught in another.

"Not exactly," she began quietly. I was with my friend Nikki. We went to the mall."

"The mall. I see. And how did you get to the mall?" asked her father.

"Her sister drove us."

"Her sister," echoed her mother. "How old is her sister?"

"Um, almost eighteen?"

Her mother gasped. "She's not even of legal age to drive you?"

Christina hung her head.

"What did you do at the mall, besides dye your hair?" asked her father in a steely tone of voice.

"Oh, we didn't dye our hair at the mall," said Christina quickly, as though it made any difference whatsoever to them where she'd done it. "We went to a movie. And then we went back to Nikki's house—not with her sister, on the bus—" she added quickly.

"The bus!" her mother cried. "By yourself!"

Her father was a little calmer. "What movie did you see?" he asked.

"Horror Sisters," whispered Christina.

Her mother closed her eyes and massaged her temples. "Let me get this straight. All this occurred *after* our discussion about how scared you get when you see horror movies. Didn't I hear you cry out in the middle of the night? You had a bad dream, didn't you?"

Christina found a bit of dried food on the tablecloth and began furiously scratching at it.

Her father banged his coffee cup down on the counter so hard, both Christina and her mother jumped. "Christina, what in the world has gotten into you?" he thundered. "Where do I begin to start listing all the rules you broke? Let's start with lying to me. Lying to your mother." He ticked them off on his fingers as he spoke. "Getting into a car with an underage driver. Going to the mall without our permission or knowledge of your whereabouts . . ."

"Okay! Okay!" said Christina. "I know what I did was wrong. But I didn't think it was all that big a deal."

"You didn't think—" began her mother. Then she started again. "Who is this Nikki?"

"Nikki Angelo. She's Mike Morris's cousin. From the pool. She's really great, and she speaks fluent French, and she can cook French food, and she's really independent, and she just got back from spending the summer in Paris, and her parents give her tons more freedom than you guys give me," said Christina, feeling her face growing hotter. "It's not like we went off and got tattoos or anything. We just saw a movie. Besides, you guys seem to have no time for me these days anyway. You're both so busy at your jobs, and going out on dates with people. I want to have a life too. And I'm getting older, in case you hadn't noticed."

Her father and mother looked at each other again. Then her mother spoke.

"Christina. I know this has been a hard time for you. It's been a hard time for all of us. But I don't like the sound of this Nikki girl. She sounds impetuous."

"And manipulative," her father chimed in.

"And," continued her mother, "it sounds like her parents have different rules for her than we do for you. But she's not my child. You are. And my responsibility is to keep you safe."

"And to impose consequences when you knowingly break the rules," added her father sternly.

Uh-oh, Christina thought. She didn't like the sound of that.

"Your father and I have discussed this," said her mother. "And we're going to ground you."

"For how long?" asked Christina tremulously.

"Until Labor Day," said her father.

Christina sank heavily into a chair. "That's almost two weeks from now," she said. "Then school's going to start. That's the whole rest of the summer."

They both nodded.

"I'll be off next week," said her mother. "We can spend some time together if that's what you really want. In the meantime, you can get some of that summer schoolwork done, which I've noticed you haven't yet begun."

"What about RSC?" Christina asked, trying not to cry.

"No RSC," said her father.

Christina stood up. She could feel the tears welling up in her eyes. She turned from them and ran out of the kitchen, up the stairs, and into her room, banging the door closed behind her.

As she sat down on her bed, a sudden thought struck her. Tomorrow. Her date with Mike. It wasn't going to happen after all. She threw herself facedown on the bed and burst into angry sobs.

Chapter Fifteen

For the rest of the morning, Christina holed up in her bedroom. She was furious with her parents and at the injustice of the world in general. For plenty of kids, what she'd done would not have been perceived as a crime at all. But Christina had to get stuck with parents who insisted on knowing where she was every second of every day.

She texted Nikki to say she was grounded. Nikki called her right away.

"How could you be grounded? You didn't do anything that bad!" she said. "I mean, please. Coloring your hair with a semipermanent glaze isn't exactly a felony."

"I know," said Christina glumly. "How about you? Did

your parents find out and get mad about the restaurant or the mall or anything?"

"Oh, pshhh," said Nikki dismissively. "Compared to my bratty little brother and my wacky older sister, they think I'm as virtuous as Mother Teresa. And if they do catch me doing something, they never stay mad for long."

Christina was starting to get a nagging feeling that her own parents might be a tiny bit right about Nikki. She was definitely—what was the word her mom had used? Impetuous. And also manipulative, as her father had said. Christina vowed to be wary of her going forward.

The next person she contacted was Mike. She texted him to say she was grounded and couldn't play miniature golf the next day. A few minutes later, her phone buzzed.

Oh, man, that stinks. What did you do, rob a bank?

She texted back:

No. I wish. At least I'd have some bags of money to show for it. They just got mad that I left RSC with Nikki the other day and didn't tell them where I was going.

A few minutes later, he replied:

Ooooh. Nikki. If you're looking for trouble, Nikki will lead you right to it.

That's just what Christina was starting to think.

Well, her parents seem a lot more understanding than mine do.

And then, to Christina's surprise, Mike texted her back:

Ya think? Uncle Vin was MAD when he got the restaurant bill.

Christina asked:

Really?

Mike replied:

Yep, and Aunt Lauren was MAD about the ruined towel. And my cousin Ben was MAD about his wrecked Red Sox shirt.

Christina was shocked. This was definitely not the way Nikki made it seem.

Oh. She made it seem like they didn't mind that stuff at all.

Mike ended the text conversation:

That's Nik. She likes to stretch the truth. Don't let her kid you—she's grounded too. Gotta go bye.

Despite her crushing disappointment at missing their date, Christina felt thrilled that Mike had had such a long conversation with her. He must really like her, even though he'd probably never see her again.

Her life was over. But still, she reread their text exchange, drumming her lips thoughtfully. Nikki had made it seem like she was allowed to do practically anything. *What else is Nikki misrepresenting to her?* she wondered.

The last person she texted was a surprise even to herself: Grace. It was just a short note:

I'm grounded. Parents mad. Life stinks.

No response. It was just as well. Grace probably disapproved of her now more than ever. *No doubt goody-goody Grace has probably never done anything she wasn't supposed to,* Christina thought bitterly.

She spent the rest of the day reading, surfing the Net, and texting, mostly with Nikki, but also with Ashley and Lindsay, who were both due back from their vacations in a few days. Luckily the rain kept up for most of the afternoon, so at least she didn't feel like she was missing out on important happenings at the club.

When she grew tired of lying there, she got up and padded over to her window. She sat down on her old kiddie stool and propped her elbows on the windowsill, staring out at the late-August rain. She could smell the mossy, damp air through the screen of her open window. She loved warm summer rains, but she could see some fallen leaves wafting downward, a reminder that fall was around the corner.

Late that afternoon she heard her mother come home, and after a few minutes there was a knock at the door. Her mother poked her head inside.

"Any interest in coming to yoga with me?" she asked.

Christina stood up. "Sure, okay," she said, and headed over to her dresser to rummage for yoga stuff. Her mother looked surprised, but also pleased.

"Great! Meet me downstairs in five minutes."

Yoga was at her mom's health club, and it turned out to be pretty fun. She was proud of herself for managing to hold the side-arm pose. A few months ago, she would have collapsed after five seconds. She was definitely stronger, and maybe a bit taller, than she'd been at the beginning of the summer. She thought she had spent most of her time at RSC lounging by the pool, not swimming in it, but she must have gotten some exercise this summer.

"Hey, Christina!" she heard someone say as she followed her mother out of the yoga room, their mats rolled under their arms. It was Jordan from RSC and his friend Joe Someone-or-other, lifting weights.

"Hey yourself!" she said back, and went over to say hello to them. Her mother sighed and kept walking.

"Where were you today?" asked Jordan as he spotted another high-school-aged boy on the bench press. "You and the rest of your crew haven't missed a day at RSC all summer."

Christina smiled at him ruefully. "I'm kind of grounded for a while. Don't ask."

Jordan smiled. "Well, try to stay out of trouble, would you?"

She laughed and waved and headed out after her mother, secretly psyched that Jordan had remembered her name.

By Friday, her anger at her parents gradually gave way to anger at herself. What she'd done had been dumb and she knew it. She could have asked her parents for permission to do most of the stuff she'd done, and most likely permission would have been granted (well, except maybe the driving-with-Jessica part). She was also angry at herself for allowing Nikki to call the shots. She could have gone to her dentist appointment and then gone to the mall, for instance. She could have requested that they see a different movie than one that gave her nightmares three nights in a row. No, she was forced to admit, she'd gotten what she'd deserved.

Friday afternoon her dad came to pick her up.

"So where to for dinner tonight?" he asked.

"How about if we go shopping at the grocery store for dinner rather than just ordering out?" Christina proposed. "And maybe we can watch a movie tonight. There's an old French film my friend recommended I see."

Her dad smiled. "I'm up for it if you are. We can stream

it after dinner. Why don't we go home and look in a cookbook and decide what we're going to make? Then we can go to the grocery store together."

Back at her dad's house, they looked in a cookbook—actually *the* cookbook, as it was the only one he owned—and planned their meal together. Then they did the shopping and came home to cook. They sautéed onion, garlic, and red pepper, and then added spices. (He didn't have cumin or coriander, but they had found allspice at the store and had agreed that it was probably a bunch of spices mixed together, so they used that.) Then they added a can of corn, a can of black beans, and finally diced turkey. Christina made the rice.

"Wow," said her dad, after trying a tentative bite. "We made turkey chili. And it is really pretty good."

"Mmm!" agreed Christina. "The rice is a little crunchy, and maybe a tiny bit burned, but the chili *is* pretty good!" They smiled at each other.

After dinner they watched the French movie, which Christina found lovely and a little puzzling. Her father dozed through the last hour of it.

Chapter Sixteen

Late afternoon on Monday, Christina lay on her bed, listlessly spinning her phone between her thumb and fore-finger. She'd gotten pretty good at it and could keep it going in a blurry circle just by tapping it along with her other hand occasionally, like a Harlem Globetrotter spin-ning a basketball on one finger. She'd certainly had plenty of time to perfect her talent. She was also scheming. In the time-honored tradition of kids who'd gotten grounded, parents *had* been known to give time off for good behavior. She vowed to make it her goal to get sprung early from her imprisonment. She would behave herself, keep doing her summer schoolwork, and be a model kid.

Sheer boredom had led to a happy outcome. For the

past few days, she'd recorded and then watched old episodes of *The French Chef*, which starred a rather hilarious woman named Julia Child. Trussing ducks and flipping omelets might be a little out of Christina's league—right now—but Julia's enthusiasm for French cooking was definitely infectious. Today she'd begun to read through some of her mother's cookbooks, paying special attention to the French-themed ones. She flipped through her little notepad, scanning it for ingredients she thought her mom might not have, and then began a shopping list for her mother.

She could hear her mom downstairs, making dinner. Reading all those recipes reminded Christina that she was getting hungry.

There was a tap at the window.

Christina whirled around. Her bedroom was on the second floor. Was it a bird? Or a squirrel or something? She stepped over to the window and pulled up the shade. A wide green smile greeted her.

Grace!

Christina peered through the screen. "What are you doing here!" she whispered to Grace.

"Came to visit," Grace whispered back. "Can you let me in, or what?"

Grinning, Christina flicked up the latches on both sides of the screen and slid it upward. She extended a hand to help Grace, who effortlessly pulled herself up to the ledge and then climbed through the space. Christina poked her head out the window to see how Grace had managed the climb. Actually, her window wasn't a full two stories up. More like one and a half. And it was a pretty easy climb up onto the stone wall, then onto the jutting-out roof above the side door, which was about four feet below the window ledge. She'd forgotten that Grace, a born gymnast, had superstrong upper-body strength. She could bang out ten pull-ups without breaking a drop of sweat, so it had probably been a breeze for Grace to make the climb.

Grace pivoted and then jumped lightly to the floor. "Where's your mom?" she whispered.

"She's down in the kitchen. Can you hear her clashing the pots and pans?"

Grace nodded and giggled.

"If she catches us, I'll be grounded until next Memorial Day," Christina whispered. But she was so happy to see Grace.

"I just came by to see how you're surviving," said Grace. "I've missed seeing you at RSC." Grace walked over to

Christina's bed and sat down. She sighed heavily, hunching her shoulders. "I also came by to, well, to say I'm sorry we had that big argument in July."

Christina came over and sat down next to her. Neither girl looked at the other. They both looked at the floor.

"I'm sorry too," muttered Christina.

"I know we've both changed and gotten older and have different interests and stuff," said Grace. "But we've been friends since we were tiny kids. I miss hanging out with you."

"Me too," said Christina. "I guess I was a little jealous of you for being a big part of the swim team right from the get-go, and for being such a good athlete. Plus you're also an artist. You're so talented."

"Well, *I* was kind of jealous of the way you seem so comfortable around everyone, and you're just so naturally pretty and fashionable and you look like you don't even try. And boys all seem to like you."

"May I remind you which of the two of us actually has a boyfriend?" asked Christina, crossing her arms and eyeing Grace mock sternly.

Grace grinned. "I suppose so. But I wouldn't say Justin and I are really, truly going out. More like we just declared that we are. But we don't really hang out all that often.

We have RSC in common, but who knows what'll happen when school starts again."

"I admit I was a little weirded out when I found out that my mom has been dating his dad." Christina made a face.

"Well, just think. If they got married, and Justin and I got married, that would make us sisters, sort of!" said Grace brightly. Her smile evaporated quickly when she saw the horror on Christina's face. "Just joking. Really." She looked like she was trying to think of a way to change the subject. "Anyway, it's not like you've been exactly ignored by the guys. I heard Mike Morris asked you out."

Christina turned to her. "So Justin told you, I guess?"

"Duh. Everyone knows. That's the kind of news that travels fast. Justin says Mike was really bummed when you got grounded. He's been swimming like ten hours a day these past few days."

Christina felt irrationally ecstatic to hear this. But she shrugged casually and said, "He's probably just being his usual self, and trying to get as much swimming in as possible before summer ends."

"I don't think so. Even Nikki can't get him to say much."

"Oh. Right. Nikki."

Both girls said nothing.

"I don't know what I did to her, but I don't think she

likes me all that much," ventured Grace. "Justin told me he and Nikki went out for, like, half a day last summer. Maybe that has something to do with her being so icy toward me."

Christina nodded. "Maybe."

"I ran into her at Dress for Less the other day at the mall," continued Grace. "She was trying on dresses. She barely said hello."

Christina's eyes widened. Nikki, at a discount clothing store, trying on dresses? Hadn't she said she never shopped at the mall? And hadn't she said—or at least implied—that she bought all her clothes at boutiques like Rive Gauche? "You know, Grace," she said, "I think Nikki can be a bit of a troublemaker. I think she enjoys stirring up problems just because it makes her life more amusing or something. And she leads you to think things about her that aren't exactly true. The more I've sat around here, with tons of time to think, the more I've decided that Nikki is better in small doses."

"You're probably right," agreed Grace.

"It's a good thing she goes to Shipton," said Christina.

"Totally," agreed Grace.

"Mel will be back in a few days," said Grace.

"Oh good. It will be nice to see her," said Christina.

Grace smiled, revealing green braces again. It struck

Christina how unimportant the color of Grace's braces really was.

They heard Christina's mom call her for dinner.

"I should go," said Grace, standing up. "But I'm really glad I came."

"Me too," said Christina, who also stood up. She opened up her arms and smiled at Grace. Grace smiled back. They hugged.

Then Grace tiptoed to the window and swung her feet around to the outside. "I'll text you," she whispered, and dropping lightly to the roof, began her climb back down.

Christina watched her ride away on her bike until she'd rounded the corner. She noticed that the shadows were already growing longer, dusk already settling in. Summer really was almost over.

When Christina came down to the kitchen a few minutes later, she found her mom tipping a steaming pot of pasta water into a colander. Garlic and oil were lightly sizzling in a pan, and chopped fresh herbs lay in a mound on the cutting board. "I have an idea," said Christina, pulling two pasta bowls from the cupboard and carrying them over to her mother.

"Uh-oh. I don't like the sound of that," her mother teased as she dumped the pasta into the oil. "What's up?"

"I was thinking that since I'm not allowed to go out these nights except with you or Dad, maybe I could invite some people over here."

Her mother frowned at her as she tossed the herbs into the pasta. "That's not quite in the spirit of being grounded, honey," she said. "You can't—"

"Wait, hear me out," Christina interrupted. "I was thinking we could invite Nathan over. With Justin and Jasper. And I can cook a French dinner. I've been watching a lot of Julia Child on TV, and she really makes it look fun."

Her mother's eyes widened with surprise, but she looked pleased. "Well! That's a bit of a different story. That sounds like a plan to me."

"And maybe Grace, too? Remember how I told you that Grace and Justin are kind of going out?"

"Of course Grace, too," said her mother. "I haven't seen her around much, and I've missed her."

Christina smiled. Maybe being grounded wasn't the end of the world.

Chapter Seventeen

The next afternoon, Christina stood in the kitchen with tears pouring down her face. Her phone buzzed. Sniffling and wiping away the tears with the back of her hand, she answered it blindly, unable to see who was calling.

"Hey, it's Nikki. How's the prisoner?"

Christina sniffed. "I'm fine," she said in a strangled-sounding voice.

"Christina. What's the matter?" Nikki sounded alarmed.

"I'm . . . I'm cutting onions. I just put them into the pan, but it was awful when I was slicing them. I'm making *soupe à l'oignon.* How do you make onion soup without tears gushing from your eyes?"

Nikki chortled. "I thought something terrible had

happened! I have no idea how to make it. I never cook. I just know how to order it in a bistro."

That surprised Christina. She had been sure Nikki had mentioned how much she loved to cook.

"So, why are you cooking, anyway?"

"We're having company tonight," said Christina. "And my mom is busy cleaning the house, so I offered to do the cooking. She went to the grocery store early this morning for me. I'm making onion soup, and then . . . hang on a second." She wiped her eyes on a dish towel and peered down at the now-splattered cookbook that was open on the counter. "And then *suprêmes de volaille* and haricots verts."

"Chicken and green beans, eh? Good for you. Better you than me. Who's coming?"

For some reason, Christina didn't think she wanted to tell Nikki who was coming. "Just friends of my mom," she said casually.

"Listen, here's why I called," said Nikki, who seemed to have lost interest in her question anyway. "I want to see if you're going to be allowed to go to the end-of-summer party on Saturday. It's going to be *très* fun."

Christina had been thinking about the party a lot. She sat down at the stool next to the kitchen counter. "Oh. The party. I'm still going to be grounded," she said. "I heard your parents were kind of mad too."

"Who told you that? Mikey? Psssh. They were a little steamed for a while, but they're over it. I was grounded for, like, ten minutes, but now they're fine."

"Been shopping lately?" asked Christina casually.

"Yep. Got an awesome dress for the party, at Rive Gauche."

Christina furrowed her brow. She knew that was probably a lie.

"So anyway, you should come to the party, even if you're still grounded," said Nikki. "We can come up with a way—especially if you're supposed to be at your dad's. Dads are easy to fool."

Christina swallowed. "I can't, Nikki," she said with a confidence she wasn't used to having around Nikki. "The last thing I need is to get into more trouble."

"Don't be so quick to say no," said Nikki brusquely. "Because my friend Becca, from Shipton, is dying to come with me to the party, and I think she has a thing for my lunkhead of a cousin and I'm not completely certain he's, shall we say, uninterested in her. I'd hate to have her, well, you know, think he's available."

Christina ran a hand through her hair and glanced at

her reflection in the toaster. She looked awful. Red-rimmed, teary eyes, wildly unbrushed hair gathered into a loose ponytail, and a smudge of flour on her cheek. Now that Nikki mentioned Mike, she started to wonder about him. He hadn't texted in two days. She had assumed he was busy, but maybe he had forgotten about her. She felt tears welling in her eyes and was pretty certain they weren't from the onions. "I'd better go," she said. "My onions are sizzling."

"Okay, well, if you want to talk, don't call the house. Just text me," said Nikki.

"Why?"

"Long story. Anyway, text me soon. Gotta go."

Christina stared thoughtfully at the phone. It certainly sounded like Nikki was in some kind of trouble with her parents. She wondered just how much Nikki was downplaying things. Maybe her dad had gotten *really* mad.

She didn't have much time to think about the party, or Mike, or who this friend of Nikki's was—Becca, was it?—and how well she knew Mike. The onions were billowing with steamy, fragrant smoke, and the water for the beans was boiling, and the chicken breasts needed dredging through flour, and the table had to be set for six. She'd gained a new respect for people who did this kind of cooking every single night.

By the time her mother was finished cleaning, wiping, sponging, and mopping the house, close to six, Christina had the beans parboiled and shocked in cold water, ready to be sautéed in butter at the last minute. She had browned the onions and added them to the broth, although they hadn't browned quite as much as she'd wanted, so the soup broth was a wan-looking light brown. Whatever. A few drops of red food coloring might darken it up. The table was set, which had taken longer than expected because she could never remember what side of the plate the forks went on and had had to Google it.

"Oh my!" exclaimed her mother. "How is my little French chef?"

"Cooking is hard," muttered Christina as she shredded cheese with the box grater.

"It can be," agreed her mom. "But it's such a nice thing to do for others. I'm so happy you proposed this plan. There's some bread and appetizer stuff in the fridge for when they arrive."

Christina had barely had time to brush her hair when she heard the bell. It was almost seven. Her mom was still changing. She hurried down the stairs and opened the door to find Justin, Jasper, and Grace on the mat, with Nathan standing behind them, holding a bottle wrapped in shiny paper with a bow. Justin and Grace both had wet, slicked-back hair, and Christina guessed they must have come right from the club.

"Hi," she said brightly, and darted a glance at Grace, who smiled. "Come on in."

The four of them trooped in and sat down in the living room on the fluffed-up couches. Nathan cleared his throat and started to say something, but then he seemed to think better of it. It occurred to Christina that he was a little shy. Luckily, her mom came down and sent her to the kitchen to pour some drinks.

The evening went about as well as she could have hoped. At first the conversation felt strained, with Christina's mother and Nathan asking the kids questions about plans for the school year. But Grace helped Christina sprinkle the cheese on the soup and then bake it, and they all came in to sit down. "This is onion soup," she announced anxiously. Nathan poked his cheese with his spoon. "It looks amazing. The cheese is so nicely browned."

Christina flushed with pleasure, and relief.

"Why's the soup red, anyway?" asked Jasper. "Did you use red onions? Ow!"

Justin had obviously stepped on his brother's foot under the table.

The chicken breasts that Christina had sautéed in huge amounts of butter tasted delicious. The green beans were a little mushy, but no one seemed to mind. Jasper talked a lot of the time about performance camp and some of the scientific journal articles he'd been reading. Grace, still shy, although not as shy as she used to be, didn't say much of anything, but Christina was glad to have her there.

"That was delicious!" said Nathan after the boys had finished clearing the plates.

"Yeah," agreed Jasper. "I hardly have room for dessert, but I'm sure I'll manage."

Christina got a stricken look on her face. She'd completely forgotten about dessert! She shot her mother a panicked look.

"I'm sure you'll be able to eat a tiny piece of raspberry tart, though, won't you, Jasper?" asked her mother, pushing back from the table and heading for the refrigerator. She pulled out a beautiful raspberry tart from the French bakery near her office and shot Christina a "gotcha covered" expression. Christina smiled gratefully at her.

After the guests had left, she and her mother finished cleaning the kitchen together. "Thanks, honey," said her mother as they turned out the lights and headed for the stairs. "That was a delightful evening, thanks to you."

"It was nice," agreed Christina. "I like cooking. It's fun."

"I appreciate how you welcomed Nathan and his boys to our house," said her mother. "It means a lot to me. And I'm glad to see you and Grace are getting to be close again."

Christina nodded and hugged her mother at the top of the stairs.

"Oh, by the way," her mom said before she went into her own room. "Nathan mentioned to me that his boys are going to an end-of-summer party at RSC this Saturday."

Christina held her breath and nodded.

"I think you've been a model of good behavior," said her mom. "No promises, but I'm going to call your father tomorrow and suggest to him that we end your grounding a few days early, and allow you to go."

Christina rushed to her mother and gave her another huge hug. "Thanks, Mom!" she said, and practically danced into her room. Her mother was the biggest hurdle. If her mom was okay with her going, her dad would certainly be.

As she brushed her teeth, she tried to imagine what it would be like to have Justin and Jasper as stepbrothers. She shuddered at the thought and put it out of her mind. No, there were more important things to think about, like what she was going to wear to the party.

Chapter Eighteen

Christina stopped just before the entrance to RSC and drew a calming breath. She was giddy with excitement. It had been way too long since she'd seen Mike, and it felt like ages since she'd seen so many of her other friends. She knew, from the flurry of recent texting, that Veronica was back from vacation and that Ashley and Lindsay were going to be there as Veronica's guests. And that Mel would be coming to the party with Grace. She smoothed down her skirt—a twirly floral print that just seemed perfect with her new nude-colored wedge sandals—and patted her hair, which she was wearing loose. She'd thought about wearing it up, the way Nikki had said Mike liked it, but the red dye just looked too . . .

stripey with it pulled back. So she'd worn it down.

She stepped inside. There were more people than she'd ever seen—many of them kids her age who she didn't recognize. White lights glittered in the trees, and an actual DJ was playing music. The pool water sparkled in the waning light. The air was cool and breezy, with just a whiff of fall on the breeze. She spotted Lindsay, Ashley, and Veronica almost at once, and raced over to see them.

"Your hair! It looks awesome!" said Ashley to Christina after the girls had all given one another big hugs.

Lisa and Jen hurried over, and everyone hugged and squealed and exchanged stories about their summers. Christina tried not to look as though she was scanning the crowd for Mike, but of course she was. Where was he? She felt someone touch her arm and turned. It was Grace. And next to her was Mel.

Mel threw her arms around Christina, and Christina hugged her back. She'd missed Mel, too. The three girls stood in a little circle, clasping one another's hands, just like old times. Then Grace looked over Christina's shoulder.

"Mike's over there," she said in a low voice, "with that girl Becca, the friend of Nikki's. I guess Nikki brought her as a guest. Don't look yet. They're sort of looking this way. Okay. Now. You can look."

Christina looked. Mike seemed to have grown two inches taller since Christina had last seen him. His hair was longer, and he had a sort of aura about him, the kind of hard-to-pinpoint air of an exceptionally attractive person who stands out from everyone else in a crowd. His appearance never ceased to take Christina's breath away.

Mike stepped to one side to put his soda down on the table, and Christina saw the girl standing next to him. Was it a girl or a fashion model? She was tall—just a few inches shorter than Mike—and willow thin, with shining chestnut-brown hair and impossibly white teeth. Her skin was smooth as porcelain, her lips full and pouty. She really did look as though she'd just stepped out of the pages of a fashion magazine. And she was holding Mike's arm and laughing at something.

"Christinaaaaaaaah!"

Christina knew that voice. It was Nikki, of course, and she was zooming toward Christina from another part of the snack area. The crowd seemed to part like the Red Sea, as Nikki made her way over, and then closed up again behind her. Some people just had that kind of power, Christina realized admiringly just before being engulfed in Nikki's fragrant hug. She could smell French shampoo and French perfume and feel the dewy softness of Nikki's bare skin, slathered, no doubt, with fancy French skin cream.

"I am so psyched that you made it here!" she said, throwing her arm across Christina's shoulders. "You look *très jolie* tonight!"

"Thanks," said Christina, trying not to turn toward Mike. Why was he ignoring her? She knew why. He had fallen for Becca. Who wouldn't?

"You hair looks gorgeous," added Nikki, reaching out to brush a strand from Christina's shoulder.

"Well, I know you said Mike liked it better up, but . . ."

"I did? Why would I say that?" said Nikki. She suddenly got sidetracked by someone over Christina's shoulder.

Christina was confused. Hadn't Nikki said before that Mike had told her he liked Christina's hair up? What else had Nikki "forgotten" or "exaggerated" or outright lied about?

"Did you see those two over there?" whispered Nikki loudly. She gestured toward Jaci and Jasper, who were standing next to each other at the punch table. "I wonder how many people have mistaken them for the caterers tonight."

They did stand out a bit, Christina was forced to agree. Both had on white shirts, buttoned all the way to the collar, and Jaci had on an unfashionably long, calf-length black skirt. Jasper wore black trousers with a sharp crease running down the front, as though someone had recently ironed them.

"I'm guessing they just performed in a concert," said Christina with a smile. "They're both pretty serious musicians. Jasper plays bassoon and Jaci plays clarinet."

"No kidding?" said Nikki, her eyes twinkling. "And all this time I thought they were in a rock band."

A song started playing, and Christina's gaze was suddenly diverted to Mike. He and Becca were dancing. She suddenly felt like a basket of wet laundry.

"Oh good, they're dancing!" said Nikki, gesturing toward Mike and Becca. "Isn't that sweet of Mikey? I was telling him how poor Becca knew no one here and that he *had* to dance with her, no offense. But I'm sure he doesn't *like* like her."

Christina resisted the strong impulse to fall onto the floor and wail like a tiny child.

"Hey, Christina!"

It was Coach Dana! Christina momentarily forgot about Mike and gave her a big hug. Then she stepped back to look at her. "Wow, Coach, you look beautiful!"

She did look pretty. Her hair, usually pulled back into a tight ponytail, hung loose and was smooth and silky, tucked behind her ears. She had on a simple sleeveless cotton tank dress that fit her perfectly and showed off her slim, athletic figure. Christina was pretty sure she even had makeup on—another first.

"Listen, Christina," said Dana. "I want to thank you for all the conniving tricks you played on Paul and me back in July. We both decided that if you hadn't interfered, we might never have gotten back together." She was referring to Christina's plan earlier in the summer to get the two coaches together, which had initially backfired but had ultimately resulted in the rekindling of their former romance.

Christina smiled. She forced herself not to look over at Mike. "You're welcome," she said. "I want you to meet my new friend Nikki Angelo. She's Mike Morris's cousin, and she's been in Paris most of the summer."

Nikki gave Coach Dana a little wave. "I've heard so much about you!" she said. "Christina didn't mention it, but I speak fluent French."

"Oh, what a fun coincidence!" said Dana, leaning into a nearby clump of people and tugging someone by the sleeve. A teenage boy emerged from the clump and came to stand next to Dana, grinning shyly. "This is Pascal, who's visiting my parents with his family. He's French! Pascal! Here's someone you can talk to in French! Nikki spent the summer in Paris."

"Enchanté," he said, shaking the hand of a somewhat stunned-looking Nikki. *"Où est-ce que tu as habité quand tu étais à Paris? Est-ce que la vie à Paris t'a plu?"*

Nikki stared at him.

Dana leaned in to hear what Nikki had to say. It suddenly struck Christina as she looked at Nikki's expression that Nikki had no earthly idea what Pascal had just asked her. For a second she was tempted to let Nikki stand there, looking stricken. But her better nature prevailed. She touched Pascal's elbow to get his attention.

"Wait, Nikki, don't answer him," she said. "I'm trying to learn French myself. Did you just ask her how long she lived in Paris and what color dog she has?"

Pascal laughed. "Almost," he said, revealing a charming French accent. "I asked her where she lived and how she liked it."

Christina laughed. "Oh well, I was almost right, wasn't I? Well, it was so nice to meet you. Come on, Nikki, let's go get a drink. I'm dying of thirst." She pulled Nikki away and toward the snack area.

Nikki clasped her arm and hugged it. "Thanks for saving me," she whispered.

"From what?" asked Christina. She decided to pretend she had no idea what Nikki was talking about. It was better that way, and so much less embarrassing for Nikki.

As they got to the punch table, they almost ran into Mike.

"Mikeeeeey!" said Nikki. "I love this girl!"

Mike looked from Nikki to Christina and grinned his half grin. "That's nice, Nik."

Christina smiled up at him. He *had* gotten taller.

"So are you officially out of trouble with your parents?" asked Mike.

Christina nodded. "I've been really, really good. I even finished my summer math packet."

"Good for you," he said. "Now you just have to stay out of trouble. The first rule to follow? Keep away from my cousin. Trouble is her middle name."

"Oh, Mikey," said Nikki, putting on a pouty face. "You can be so mean to me. I hope you were nice to my friend Becca."

Mike shifted uncomfortably. "Yeah, she's cool."

Christina tried to keep her features arranged in a neutral expression, but her insides were roiling. Why had Nikki brought Becca along to the party?

"You'd better be sure to ask her for another dance," said Nikki. "Like I said, she doesn't know a soul here, poor thing."

They all looked across the party at Becca. She was

surrounded by boys. *She does not appear to be suffering from loneliness,* Christina thought drily.

"Well, right now I thought maybe I'd see if *you* wanted to dance," said Mike to Christina. "I'm pretty terrible at dancing. Don't hate me if I step on your feet."

Christina smiled and nodded, and she followed him out to the dance floor. Out of the corner of her eye she could see Nikki, standing alone and watching them.

They danced three times in a row. When the DJ finally put on a slow song, Mike raised his eyebrows in a question, and Christina nodded. He stepped close to her and somewhat awkwardly put his arms around her so they were just barely grazing the small of her back. She almost didn't dare touch him, for fear she'd get an electric shock, the way you get when you shuffle across the carpet in your socks and then touch someone. But she made herself put her arms around his shoulders. She was sure he could hear her heart thudding like a big bass drum.

"So Nikki's friend Becca seems nice," she said tentatively. She could smell his manly body spray.

Mike scoffed. "Whatever. Nikki made me dance with her, saying the poor, lonely girl didn't know anyone here. Nikki can be fun, but I swear she just gets bored and tries to stir up drama just to amuse herself."

Christina smiled and shuffled just a bit closer to him.

"So maybe now that you're out of Parent Prison, we could, like, meet at the mall or something sometime?" he said.

"That sounds good," said Christina, trying not to scream "YES!!!" at the top of her lungs.

Before they could dance a fifth time in a row, Mike got dragged away by Justin and a couple of others from the boys' team to go see Coach Paul. Grace and Justin had been dancing, but Grace joined Christina as they watched the boys go.

"Eeeee!" Grace squealed as she put her hands on Christina's shoulders and bounced up and down, her eyes shining with delight. "I saw you and Mike dancing together! You danced a *lot*! Even a *slow* dance!"

Christina giggled and did a little dance step in place. "He stepped on my toes about seventeen times, but who cares, right?" It was so nice to have Grace back in her life again, she realized suddenly.

"This is fun," said Grace.

"Yeah, it's a nice party," said Christina. "Listen, I'm really glad you came over to my house that day. It was great to talk to you."

"Yeah, I'm glad I did too," said Grace.

They watched Nikki grab Becca from the midst of her group of boys and propel her out to the dance floor, where the two of them joined a bunch of other girls who were dancing in a big group.

"Nikki's wearing the dress I saw her trying on the other day," remarked Grace.

"Hmm," said Christina. "She told me she got it at some fancy boutique. Sometimes I wonder if she thinks telling the truth is optional."

Grace nodded, keeping her face neutral. "Yep. You could say that." By now Nikki was dancing, this time with a boy Christina didn't know; he must be from another swim club, she figured. He was a good dancer. So was Nikki, for that matter. A space opened up all around them, as though everyone in the crowd knew these two had superior talents and deserved more space than others.

The song ended and Nikki approached them, her face slightly flushed with exertion, her eyes bright. She looked stunning. "So, Christina, did you hear the news that everyone's talking about?"

"No, I don't think so," said Christina. She looked at Grace. "Did you, Grace?"

Grace shook her head.

A flicker of annoyance passed across Nikki's face.

Christina knew what it meant. Nikki didn't want to talk in front of Grace. But Christina ignored the message.

"So, what's the news?" she asked.

"I'm going to your school this year. Starting on Tuesday I'll be a Lincoln middle schooler!" said Nikki. "Isn't that awesome? I know. You're speechless. Well, I finally convinced my parents to let me go to public school. The soccer is so much better there. And soccer is so my sport. I can't wait, and I'm so excited that I already know so many people there. Oops, gotta go. Kyle is waving me over to dance."

And she twirled away like an autumn leaf.

"Why are you both opening and closing your mouths like goldfish?" asked Jaci, who had just joined them.

Grace and Christina looked at each other, wide-eyed. Neither seemed able to speak.

"Okay, well, I'll leave you two to your deer-in-the-headlights moment," said Jaci with an amused smile. "I'm off to dance with Jasper, who just rocked the house in our concert." She headed off to join Jasper on the dance floor.

Grace and Christina watched Jaci and Jasper dancing together, ballroom-style, seemingly oblivious to the fact that no one else was dancing that way.

Christina found her voice first. "Did you hear what Nikki just said?"

"About how she's going to be coming to our school this year? Yes."

"That *is* what she said, isn't it?"

"Mmm-hmm."

Neither spoke for a moment.

"How much of what Nikki says do you think we should believe?" asked Grace. "I mean, do you think she even went to France this summer, or did she really spend her vacation in a dusty cabin in the woods somewhere?"

Christina shrugged. "I'm not sure. She told me she wants to train to be a chef. And that she speaks fluent French. And that she buys her clothes at fancy stores. And that her parents let her do all kinds of stuff, but in fact they actually don't let her."

"So we don't know if what she just told us is true or false, is that what you're saying?" asked Grace.

"Right," replied Christina.

"I guess we'll find out on Tuesday. And either way, we have an exciting year to look forward to," said Grace at last.

Christina nodded. "And either way, I'm sure we haven't heard the last of Nikki," she added. Grace giggled as the two girls joined the rest of their friends as they danced away one of the last nights of their amazing summer.

Growing up, Cassie Waters spent every waking moment of every summer at her swim club (which was conveniently located at the end of her street). These days Cassie lives in the suburbs of New Jersey, writing and editing books, hanging out with friends, and having lots of fun. Over the years, Cassie has written dozens of books, but the Pool Girls series is nearest and dearest to her heart. She doesn't make it to the pool nearly as often as she would like these days, but she is still very good friends with the girls she used to hang out with at her swim club.

Ready for more drama?

Read all about the confessions of Madison Hays in

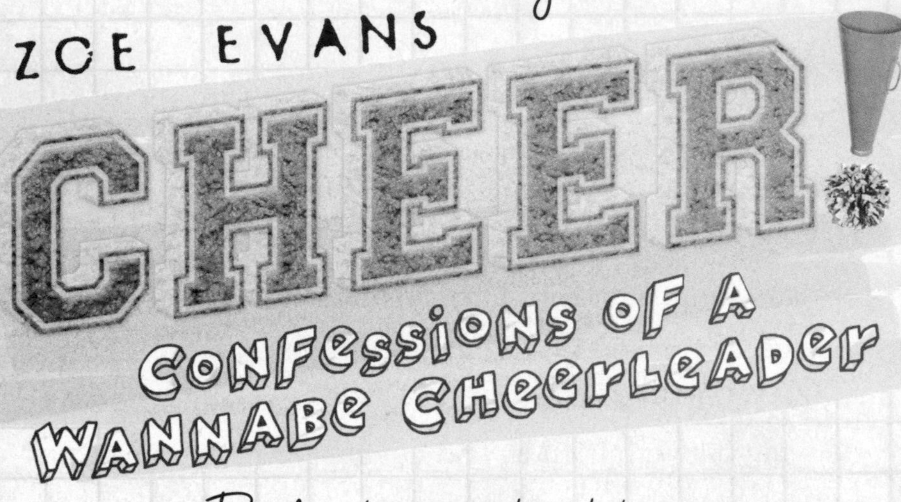

Read on for a sneak peek from . . .

. . . and look for more Cheer books at your favorite store!

Monday, November 15

After Grizzly practice, Port Angeles School locker room

Spirit Level:

Ready and (sort of) OK!

The gym at Port Angeles School was even noisier than usual this afternoon when I met up with my cheer co-captain, Jacqueline Sawyer, to lug the boxes that had arrived at my house earlier this morning over to the rowdy group of cheerleaders in their designated corner. I couldn't wait to show the Titans the new uniforms I designed for their team—for **REALZ** this time. Well, I mean, I **DID** design them the last time—it's just that there was an itsy-bitsy mix-up when Jacqui submitted the designs to the uniform company. See, she kinda put her own spin on them so that when the Titans got their new uniforms, instead of saying "Titans" on the shirts, it read "Tight Ends." This was Jacqui's way of getting back at her old teammates for kicking her off the squad, but it also put me in a totally awkward position.

Here's what the uniforms looked like when I first handed the sketch over to Jacqui.

And here's what they looked like after Jacqui had her revenge.

Ridiculous!! It looked like a football uniform married a cheerleader uniform and then had a baby uniform that went onto the discount rack at Filene's Basement. Total fashion faux pas.

Anyway, I made good on my promise to get the uniforms right this time, and thankfully, Jacqui stayed out of my way. Well, the truth is, she's back to (kinda) being friends again with Katie Parker, Titan head cheerleader and all-around Miss Perfect.

"Watch out, Grizzlies coming through!" cried Hilary Cho when she spotted us. Then she did a little roar, like a bear. Ha-ha. Get it? Grizzly Bears? Like I haven't heard that one before.

So, Hilary is the third girl in what my friends and I like to call the "Triumvirate" of the Titan cheerleaders: Katie Parker, Clementine Prescott, and Hilary Cho. Hilary pretty much just goes along with whatever Katie and Clementine think is cool. She's a total sheep. Baa, baa.

I hate it when the Titans get all snotty like that. I mean, the Grizzly Bears are cheerleaders too! OK, so we're kind of at the bottom of the cheerleading food chain.

The Grizzlies were formed because the school felt that no one should be turned away from wanting to participate in school-spirit-related activities. Anyone who doesn't make the cut for Titan tryouts automatically gets to be on the Grizzly squad. Hooray! So that's where we come in: We are the voice of the uncoordinated. We also come in handy when the Titans are so busy competing to get to Nationals that they can't cheer at our school's games. I mean, who else would cheer for debate team, chess club, or math league?

But still, there's no need for people like Hilary to rub it in our faces.

I'm far from uncoordinated, but I know I'm not quite Nationals material. Still I'm a way better cheerleader than anyone on my team (except for Jacqui, obvs, but she **WAS** a Titan once, after all). My ultimate dream is to be a Titan. I just keep hoping that if I practice harder, learn the Titans' killer choreography, and hit every stunt, I'll be good enough to wear one of the uniforms I worked so hard designing for their squad.

"So, what's with the boxes?" asked Clementine, Triumvirate Member #2. "Make it quick. We're bugging out." (Ugh. Being on Clementine's bad side is never a good idea. Ever. She can cut you with just one nasty look, seriously. Once, she looked at a seventh grader funny and the girl broke out in hives!! For realz.)

I explained that I was about to present her and her team with new uniforms. Of course this got Clementine's attention. (Anything having to do with Clementine usually does.) She knelt down beside the box I'd opened to grab one of the plastic-wrapped uniforms.

"Huh, this doesn't look like a disaster," she said, checking out the skirt appreciatively. This was a high compliment coming from Clementine. She smoothed the skirt against her spray-tanned legs. "Ooh, and it's short, too!"

Jacqui started opening another box just as Katie came over to us looking flustered.

"Oh, good! The uniforms!" she said, tightening her ponytail nervously. "Hey, thanks, Madison. We've got to make this quick, though. We're starting to get ready for the Regional Qualifier today."

Sigh. The Regional Qualifier. As soon as she breathed those words, I had this insane feeling of jealousy. Which I **HATE**. But I would kill to be in one of those competitions. The Regional Qualifier is, like, one of **THE** most important ones of the year. If your team places in it, then you get to go on to the Regional Championships. Without qualifying for Regionals? You can kiss Nationals (i.e., the holy grail of cheer competitions) good-bye.

"These are amazing!" squealed Katie, holding a uniform out in front of her. "OMG, Madison. Loves!"

She was literally smiling from ear to ear. Jacqui gave me a little wink.

"Awesome. Glad you guys like 'em," I said.

T.G. I'm **BEYOND** relieved. I mean, can you even imagine what would've happened if she'd, like, hated them? I couldn't mess up **AGAIN**!! Not with my future team captain (fingers crossed! ☺). Also, Katie and I have become more friendly just recently. I bet if I hadn't made these uniforms look perfect, she would've gone right back to ignoring me. No, thank you!

"Hey, Coach!" shouted Clementine. "Look!" She pointed to the boxes of uniforms.

Coach Whipley glanced in our direction, then gave Clementine the thumbs-up. (Obviously uniforms aren't a big deal to her. Hmph!) Then she started barking orders about permission slips and choosing roommates for the overnight stay at the competition site. Jacqui and I took that as our cue to leave and headed over to the Grizzly corner of the gym.

As we walked to our mat to start stretching I asked Jacqui if the Titans always get this freaked before big competitions.

"Well, the Titans don't take any competition lightly," she said with a laugh. "But I heard that this year a lot of schools are nervous about the qualifier because the judges are supposed to be pickier than ever."

"Hmm," I said, starting on some neck rolls. "So, how often are the rumors true?"

Jacqui looked off beyond the bleachers behind me, thinking. "Um, well, last year there was a rumor that teams would be judged superharshly on their dance routines, and in the end even the best dancers didn't place as well as they usually do. So . . ." She shrugged.

"Do you think the Titans really have anything to worry about?" I asked.

"Yeah," said Jacqui. "They don't have *me* on the team anymore." She laughed. "No, but seriously, even though they freak out, they always place."

Just then my mom—I mean, Coach Carolyn—walked into the gym, followed by the rest of my teammates. Sometimes I wonder how I got so "lucky" (yeah, right) that I get to hang with Mom not only at home, but at school, too. To what do I owe this honor?! I'm just glad she didn't get an office here. That would have been **THE END**. I feel bad thinking this, but sometimes I wish my mom was more normal. Normal moms probably can't say that they were homecoming queens, prom queens, cheerleading captains—basically every popular title a person can have. And it's hard to be on the loser cheerleading team knowing that Mom's cheer skills were legendary at my school. So when Jacqui convinced me that Mom should be the Grizzly coach, it was pretty rough. At first, all Mom could talk about was cheer,

cheer, cheer. Oh, **AND** she was constantly butting in about Grizzly stuff that wasn't really her problem. But ever since we had a big talk about it, I think it's working out pretty well. Except for when she calls me "sweetie" at practice.

"Hey, sweetie," said Mom, ruffling my hair when she walked past me.

Grrr.

"Hi, sweeeetie!" teased Matt Herrington, one of the two ex-football-jocks on our squad.

Ian McClusky, his partner in crime, chuckled behind him.

I gave them both a dirty look. I think Matt and Ian might actually have some cheer potential, even though they're total clowns. Their upper-body strength would make them really good bases for partner stunts—that is, if they didn't get hysterical every time they had to lift one of us girls. Morons.

"As captains, you know we can easily make you do, like, a hundred push-ups just for disrespecting us," said Jacqui. This seemed to quiet them down.

I started the team on our usual warm-up—some good stretches on the mat for our calves, hips, and hamstrings—and then back bends.

During a break I told the team about the Titans

going to the Regional Qualifier.

"Is zis competitive vdt you call 'beeg'?" asked Katarina Tarasov in her typical botched-up version of the English language. I heart Katarina a ton because she's got mad gymnastics skillz, which definitely helps bring the Grizzlies up a notch.

"Yeah, it's one of the bigger competitions of the season," my mom said. "It determines whether they'll go to Regionals. I can guarantee you'll be seeing the Titans work even harder than normal for the next few weeks." She nodded to the corner of the gym where the Titans were practicing their perfect-looking jumps.

"Ok, guys, rest time is over," I told them. "If you ever want to get your jumps to look like theirs, then partner up."

I saw that Mom was watching us practice, but she had a funny look on her face—like she was totally thinking about something else. Then it hit me! I know that look. It's the look she has whenever she has something brutal in mind for me—or in this case, the Grizzlies. Something is brewing in Mom Brain. Why do I have a feeling it's not going to be pretty?